FABULOUS

Peculiar Ground

NON-FICTION
Cleopatra
Heroes
The Pike: Gabriele D'Annunzio

FABULOUS

Stories

Lucy Hughes-Hallett

HARPER

An Imprint of HarperCollinsPublishers

FABULOUS. Copyright © 2020 by Lucy Hughes-Hallett. All rights reserved. Printed in the United States of America. No part of this book may be used or reproduced in any manner whatsoever without written permission except in the case of brief quotations embodied in critical articles and reviews. For information, address HarperCollins Publishers, 195 Broadway, New York, NY 10007.

HarperCollins books may be purchased for educational, business, or sales promotional use. For information, please email the Special Markets Department at SPsales@harpercollins.com.

Originally published in Great Britain in 2019 by 4th Estate, an imprint of HarperCollins Publishers.

FIRST U.S. EDITION

Library of Congress Cataloging-in-Publication Data has been applied for.

ISBN 978-0-06-294009-4

20 21 22 23 24   LSC   10 9 8 7 6 5 4 3 2 1

For Dan, with love

Each of these modern stories
is a variation (a very free one) on a much older tale.
The original fables are summarised
at the end of the book.

CONTENTS

ORPHEUS

There was no forewarning.

She was in the park with her friend.

Every Wednesday they went, with their dogs. 'What do you say to each other?' he asked. She couldn't answer. But he knew that they talked all the way round.

Once he went looking for them. There was something he was worried about. Something that couldn't wait until she got back, at least that's what he thought. He saw them coming towards him between the silver birches and she was talking, hands in the pockets of her old velvet coat, head down watching her feet, talking non-stop. When she looked up and saw him she waved, and after that it was her friend who was talking, looking at him, as she did so, in a way he thought rude. When they came up to him he explained about the thing. Was it the heating? He wanted her to hurry home with him, but she didn't seem to care about it. She wasn't a worrier the way he was. Sometimes he found her insouciance maddening.

Anyway, that was a while ago. But then she was out with her friend again and the earth cracked open and an arm reached up from the chasm and dragged her down.

The friend, she was called Milla, came and rang the door-bell. He could hear her over the intercom but he couldn't understand what she was saying. He could have just pressed the little button, but he didn't want her coming in for some reason – he'd get annoyed with Milla, the way she was always wanting his wife to go out with her and leave him on his own – so he took his keys like he always did, in case, and went down the stairs quite slowly. Through the stained glass he could see Milla jerking around, and he could hear the bell ringing and ringing upstairs in the flat. He opened the front door. He'd probably been asleep. That would be why he hadn't noticed she was late back, and why he wasn't sensible enough to let Milla in with the little knob.

Milla said, 'Oz, I'm so sorry. Oz, Eurydice's . . . She's in St Mary's. I'll take you. Let's go and get your coat.'

The terrible arm dragged Eurydice out of the light. She, who had always slept with a lamp left on in the corridor because darkness pressed against her eyes and smothered her sight. She, who would fuss about restaurant tables, who always wanted the one by the window. She, who would shift her chair around the room throughout the day, dragging it six inches at a time to be always in the patch of sunlight. She sank into blackness. She was obliterated.

Milla didn't see it happen. Oz saw it as they drove to the hospital. He saw it over and over again. He saw the hand slip-ping itself around Eurydice's knees as a snake might wrap itself around its prey. He saw it descend on her from above and lift her by her hair so that the skin of her gentle face was pulled tight over sharp bones. He saw it grasp her around the hips and heave her up, head and feet flopping down undignified. Fee Fi Fo Fum and down she goes. Into the crevasse she went, into the valley of death, into the foul mouth.

Where is she? He kept asking and asking. Milla was patient with him. Milla said, 'She's in St Mary's. We're on our way there. We'll see her very soon.' 'I know, Oz, I do too, but the doctors are with her. We just have to sit and wait.' 'I don't know how long, but the nurse will tell us as soon as she can.' 'I'll get you a cup of tea, shall I?' 'Don't drink it yet, it'll be hot.' 'I'll wait outside. Here. This gentleman will help you.' 'She's in the Greenaway Ward. We'll see her in a minute or two.' 'In here.' 'She's here, Oz. Look. Here she is.' But Eurydice was gone.

What had been left lying among the pliable blades of coming daffodils was something as frail and pretty and futile as the feathers from a plucked bird. He was grateful to Milla for caring so much about it. He knew she was right – the conventions governing human civilisation required them to pick the remnant up, and rush to find help for it, and keep watch by it – but it was no longer Eurydice, no longer his wife. He saw the hands, dry and pale, with the tiny wart at the base of the third finger on the right, and her grandmother's pearl ring on the middle finger on the left, and the broken nail she had complained about as she was putting on her scarf to go out that morning and the nail caught in the woolly stuff. They were her hands, but she had left them, along with her thinning hair and scaly elbows (I'm like an old tortoise, she said, when she felt them) and the ankles which still, when she wore black tights or even more when she was bare legged in summer, were worth showing off. These things had been hers, but they failed to contain her, to keep her safe.

Gluck has him singing at the moment of loss. A lament, generalising from the particular, meditating upon lovelessness and how it annuls life's meaning. Stuff like that. Monteverdi was wiser. Monteverdi asks him only to sing a word that is barely a word even. '*Ahimè*'. A sigh. A sigh which brings the lips together, which says mmmm's the word from now on for evermore, and then relents into that plangently accented vowel.

He had a remarkable counter-tenor voice. The critics said Suave Silvery Ethereal Limpid. When he was young he was afraid women would think he was gay, or weird, because his voice was as ungendered as an angel's, but he needn't have worried.

All that afternoon he sang. He felt too shaky to stand but his powerful lungs drew in air and converted it into music. He was a clarion. Milla tried to hush him but he didn't even know that he was singing, so how was he to know that he should stop? They gave him a chair and placed him by the bed where they said Eurydice was lying, but she wasn't there.

He could see her neck, and the softly puckered skin where it met her shoulders. He knew that part of her so well – so well – but this afternoon it was no longer hers. She'd left it behind, as she left clean hankies in the pocket of his coat when she borrowed it. Her favourite mug, the colour of violets, upturned by the sink. Clues as to her presence. He tried to tell one of the nurses how touched he was to see that piece of her neck, how much it reminded him of her, but the nurse thought he was worried that she might be cold, and pulled up the blue blanket so that even that memento of her was hidden from him.

The face was a perfect replica of her face. He touched it very lightly from time to time and felt the warm dryness of it, and he ran his fingers over her eyelids, and felt the fluttering movement beneath, just as though she was still there.

Milla left and other people came. A young couple, Eurydice's nephew and his wife. They said to each other, 'Shouldn't we take him home?' When he heard that he sang louder and for a while they let him be. When it was night, though, they led him down the long luminous corridors and out into the spangled dark.

They fed him and stayed the night in the spare room, her workroom, and when he sat up in bed and sang again the young woman came, wrapped in Eurydice's cashmere shawl, and lay down on his bed beside him and held his hand and said, 'You need to sleep. Sleep now. In the morning we'll see if we can bring her back.' He couldn't remember how to sleep but he lay down when the niece made the pillows right for it, and then the singing moved from his chest to his mind, and all night his head rang with sounds as clear and dazzling as sunlit seawater seen by one swimming an inch or two under.

For most of his life he had been a middle-aged person's kind of artiste. He sang, with his friend Marcia accompanying him, at the Maltings, the Wigmore Hall, places like that. He used to wear formal dark clothes, or sometimes, for Handel, silk frock-coats and breeches. He liked the costumes. He took a luxurious pleasure in the heaviness of lined and interlined satin. He enjoyed being someone other than himself. Then he accepted an invitation to sing with a group of clever young people who told him how much they admired him. He hadn't much liked the music but he let his voice glide like quicksilver over the rough ground of the drums and sharp peaks of the electric guitars. Less than a week from first approach to recording studio, but afterwards strangers began to talk to him in shops. They were amazed, they said, by what he could do with his voice. As though they had no idea how often he'd done far better things, as though they had never heard of *coloratura*. 'Enjoy it,' said Eurydice. 'Don't grouch.'

There was a concert in Hyde Park. He wore ear-plugs – his hearing was precious. He stood at the back of the stage harmonising softly until it was time for his aria (they didn't call it that). His voice, amplified, offended him with its coarseness. With the lights changing colour in his eyes, he couldn't see. But he could sense the shuffle and sway of thousands of people on their feet. This is dangerous, he thought. He detested demagoguery. Afterwards he shut himself away to work on Purcell.

The next morning he woke early and slipped out of the flat without waking the young couple, even though the niece was still stretched out on his bed. When your life's work is making exactly calibrated sounds and fitting them together in sequences whose tempi and tones you modify and adjust and rehearse and rehearse and rehearse, when you do that, day after day, your ear constantly straining to detect and eliminate the subtlest infelicities, you learn not to clatter about.

People were always taking his arm, but they did so to steer him, not because he needed to be propped up. He had piano-player's shoulders and the leg muscles of one who could stand stock still throughout a recital. He let himself be steered. He'd learnt long ago that it was wise to abdicate power over tedious matters to another. To Eurydice. But that didn't mean he was feeble.

There were a lot of elderly men around the hospital. They hovered near it. They stretched out on benches under the concrete overhangs. They leant against its walls to smoke. They went tentatively into the halls and waiting areas. As they ventured indoors they were wary but this late on in the night shift no one had the will to shoo them away. Or the heart. There were chairs in the hospital, and there was light. Hard plastic chairs and harsh shadeless light, but beggars can't be . . . Once inside they could attend to their feet. Their feet were of great concern to them. They cosseted them. They swaddled them in cloth. They went into the washrooms and anointed them with warm water and disinfectant gel. Some of them had big trainers, shiny white shoes made for athletes, but here nobody sprang, nobody leapt.

He went among them, another suppliant. He passed softly through the dim entrance hall. The floor was hard, so that to walk on it was to make noise. The low ceiling was insulated with white stuff that swallowed the noise up. Sound. Smother. A closed system. He nodded to the gatekeeper, a woman who glanced at him briefly and saw that he was admissible, and let him go by. He was, as he always was, neat, and he stepped carefully over the slick grey ground.

* * *

He went upstairs to where they had said she was, to the bed where her abandoned body had lain, but there was nothing there. Not an empty bed even. Nothing. On other beds women slept, pale, their hipbones and feet making ridges and peaks in the thin cellular blankets. They snored or muttered and tiny sharp lights blinked.

'You're looking for your wife.' A nurse. Male. African. Very large.

'She was here.' He no longer felt certain he had come to the right place.

Amidst the dimness the nurse sat in a cone of light.

'There were concerns. She's under observation. She'll be going to imaging shortly.'

'Can I see her?'

'Best to wait here, sir. She'll come back here.'

All that day he sat in the ward, by the window. The nurse gave him his chair again and brought him a plastic pot of yoghurt. The sun rose showily, unfurling streamers of lurid orange cloud while the sky faded. No sound from the outer world passed through the sealed glass. Visitors arrived. A Frenchman, with clever eyes and pendulous doggy jowls, came and sat beside his thin wife, and the two of them worked together on a crossword. A woman whose soft arms and shoulders billowed around her apologised and apologised. Sorry for the trouble. Sorry for the moans she couldn't help but make. Sorry for the retching that from time to time possessed her. The nurses tended to her, unshaken alike by her pain and the pointlessness of her sorry sorry sorry.

Milla found him. 'We were frantic. We didn't know where you'd got to.' As though he might have been anywhere else but here. Here, waiting for Eurydice. Here, watching by the crack down which she had been dragged into the underworld. Milla bustled about and asked questions, and went on a long excursion into another part of the hospital and returned to tell him what he already knew. Concerns. Imaging. Wait here.

Milla was really very good. He'd always liked being taken charge of by bossy people. When Eurydice seized his hand long ago and said, 'You. You'll dance with me, won't you?' and looked in his face so that he knew at once that she could see him, all of him, and found parts of what she saw absurd and other parts precious, he had said 'Yes', said it with every fibre of his being, every droplet of his being, every inter-molecular current and electro-magnetic charge and neural pulse of his being, with all the ardour that was in him, with his whole heart.

Milla was walking towards him, with two people he didn't know, both in uniform. She squatted down beside his chair, rocking awkwardly on her high heels. Why on earth did women wear those things? Eurydice never did.

Milla said something. Her mascara had smeared all around her eyes. What she said was incomprehensible.

The floor gaped open and down he flew.

*   *   *

God almighty, what a racket.

He'd had a scan once. He'd taken off his proper clothes and, dressed in a penitent's thin smock, had been borne away into the white enamelled throat of a machine. The noises it made were rhythmic and various. It roared and chugged and emitted long dragging sounds that had no trace of voice in them, because a voice can belong only to a being, and this thing was devoid of intention, devoid of life. He hadn't been afraid then, just very lonely because Eurydice hadn't come with him, and he'd been collected enough to think, You could do something with this. This is interesting. Why hasn't a composer picked up on this? Perhaps someone has. This is imaging. This is the sound of a thing which looks at you without passion or compassion or even dispassion and – oddly enough – it's musical.

Now, as he descended into the rocky innards of the earth in search of his Eurydice, he heard that music amplified a thousandfold. He heard matter grinding itself as it shifted. Ancient masses cooling, heating, expanding, collapsing. The fearsome noise of the inanimate on the move. He sang into it. His eyes were open on absolute darkness. He felt speed but could measure it only by the pressure of air against his chest, and by the void he sensed opening behind him like unfurled wings. Into the darkness he fired his voice. The uproar of rock and magma gave him his baseline. His song arced over it, flashing.

From morn to noon he fell, from noon to dewy eve, and all that time he saw no one, and breathed air that smelt of coal, and there was no dew, only clamminess, and then he was in a room, or a cavern – a finite space at least with black walls, and shaded lights that set the blackness glittering – and there was Eurydice, not the limp and pitiful residue that had lain in the hospital bed, but Eurydice herself, smiling at him with her slightly crooked mouth.

'This is a bit drastic,' she said. She disliked theatrical gestures.

'I had to come,' he said. 'I'm no good without you.'

'Hey ho,' she said, and he could see her bracing herself to resume the business of being loved.

There were other people there, two of them. Doctors presumably. When Orpheus stepped forward to take Eurydice's hands something prevented him, an obstruction in the air. The man said, 'This isn't really possible you know.'

The other one, the woman, came and took him by the arm. Her face looked red and blotched, cross, but when she touched him he felt that her hands were kind. It was something he had discovered in his dealings with the medical profession, the efficacy of the laying-on of hands. 'The thing is,' she said, in a reasonable voice, 'you're actually still alive. It's most unusual.'

Eurydice watched and smiled but she didn't move towards him. There was something vague about her, or maybe it was only that his eyes had been so exhausted by darkness that what they saw was half blotted out. The woman led him over to where the man was and they all three sat, and Eurydice was there with them – there, but not entirely there.

'I can't do without her,' said Orpheus.

'A lot of people in your situation feel that way,' said the man.

'We're not denying the existence of grief,' said the woman. 'We know how challenging it can be, especially to those who are of a certain age.'

'My life is founded on her love,' said Orpheus. 'On loving her.'

The woman stroked his hand.

'You have friends,' said the man. 'You have intellectually stimulating work. You have an adequate level of financial security. I know these things may seem paltry in the light of what has happened, but our experience tells us that you will gradually recover your enthusiasm for them.'

They both talked like that. They offered counselling. They spoke at length about the importance of maintaining social contacts, about taking walks on a regular basis and eating sensibly. All the time he was looking at Eurydice and she was looking at him. She seemed amused. Often at parties they would catch each other's eyes like this – he signalling 'Time to go?' and she signalling back 'Come on, you old spoilsport. Give it a bit longer.' She was clearer now, fully in focus, but he could see the blackness of the rock-face through her insubstantial frame.

'You'll find a regular sleep-pattern is vitally important,' said the man. 'We can help you there. Hypnotics are really very effective nowadays and the adverse side-effects are negligible.'

'Have you ever considered taking a cruise?' asked the woman.

Orpheus didn't answer them. He didn't look at them. He fixed his eyes on Eurydice's and he took a breath and he sang.

* * *

They flew. The music lifted them. He could no longer see her but that was only because the darkness was, once more, absolute. She was definitely there. He could feel the soft secret parts of her body that he knew as no one else did, the valleys flanking her hip-bones, her earlobes, the backs of her knees. The sense of them was on his fingertips. He could smell her hair. Her being warmed his back. Always, when he woke in the morning, he knew before he opened his eyes whether she was still in the bed. It wasn't that they slept entangled as they had when they were young. Their bed was wide, and they kept to their own sides of it, but always there was that warmth which is not only bodily – the warmth of another person's presence. Breathing makes a sound, but it also makes a vibration in the air. She was there. She was following him. Her following powered his flight and his song powered hers.

My song is love unknown

He sang hymns in the bath. He used to sing them on his bicycle before his knee seized up. His singing life had begun in church when he was a child. The lady who drove the library van smiled at him from the choir stalls and he thought she was inviting him to fly up with her, so when she sent her voice looping above the others – high, higher – he followed her with his own. Afterwards his parents apologised – Honestly, I don't know how he even knows the descant – but the library lady smiled again and said to the vicar, 'I think we've found our soloist for "Once in Royal", haven't we?' He didn't know what she was talking about. He was seven years old. After that he sang with the lady every Sunday. The most useful part of my entire education, he'd tell interviewers. Forget about God; we have to keep the churches open so young people get a chance to sing.

> But O! my Friend,
> My Friend indeed,
> Who at my need
> His life did spend.

He had no intention of spending his life for Eurydice, or anyone else for that matter, but he had to get her out of there, and himself. They had to keep rising. In the dark room he had held her gaze, because he thought that his seeing her made her visible. Now, with the same dogged fixity, he concentrated his will on a point of light an immense distance above them. He was tired. He couldn't remember why he was in this dark place, why his wife was clinging to him, so heavy, so heavy, but he knew he must keep his eyes on that light, must keep his voice sounding out, however dry his throat or short his breath, must keep ascending on a stream of silver sound – limpid, ethereal, suave as upwardly flowing milk – leaping towards the light.

He was so angry when they resuscitated him that the nurses – two men – backed off momentarily, accustomed as they were to dealing with the desperate, before buckling-to again and holding him down. Milla said, 'We nearly lost you too. Can't have that, Oz. What would poor Dodie do?' Dodie was the dog. He hadn't given her a thought. Milla must have handed her over to some friend or neighbour. What the fuck made her think he cared buggeration about the dog? He couldn't give a shit about the dog. He'd never liked it.

A nurse said, 'Don't let him upset you, love. It's shock. And the dementia. He'll be the perfect gentleman again once he's calmed down.' He heard as from a long way off. He fought. He shouted. He wanted them all to be upset.

He had so nearly made it. His song had amazed him, so beautiful it was, and so potent. As deep water will not accept a bladder full of air, as it forces it back up to rejoin its own element, so the darkness had repulsed him. With music streaming from his mouth he was luminous. He was swept back up into the light. But he was swept alone. His power to save Eurydice depended on his being independent of her. He mustn't turn to her for help. He mustn't turn at all. But, with his attention fixed on the gleam, he had forgotten whom he was carrying. Tossing in the current of song he became bewildered. He didn't know what he was doing here. He knew there was something he needed to worry about. Was it the heating? Something like that. He took his eye off the circle of light. He looked around. He had lost his sense of purpose. He needed a clue, a cue. He looked back.

The darkness had thinned. He could see dimly. He could see Eurydice. She was wearing a headscarf tied under the chin, the way she used to when he first knew her. Again, there was that warmth. She looked exasperated as she caught his eye and then he could see her bracing herself again. She moved her hands as though she was smoothing out a tablecloth. She said, 'Never mind, darling.' He surged on, helpless, while she drifted and spun a while, and then began to sink, so slowly that she seemed to be barely moving, back into the murk.

'You couldn't have saved her,' said Milla. 'Nobody could.' Oz knew that. He was a rational human being, except when he was tired or flustered. He knew that a hospital was a place from which one couldn't count upon returning. He just wished that he could have died too.

His voice was not what it had been of course, but it was still a marvellously affecting instrument. A group of young women who performed folk songs *a capella* invited him to join them on tour. On stage they deferred to him. In the B-and-Bs they fussed over him, and made him hot drinks and lent him their pashminas to wrap around his throat. Reviewers were snide. 'What's happened to him?' asked his agent. 'Has he lost his marbles?' 'Well yes, he has,' said Milla. 'He's also lost his wife.'

ACTAEON

He was quite a bit younger than me, than most of us actually, but he called us his 'boys'. Looking back on it, I'm surprised no one protested, not even Eliza. 'Let's do it, boys,' he'd go, at the end of the Friday meeting. 'Let's nail those sales.' When we went for a drink (which we did weekly, it was the next piece of the Friday warm-up), Acton talked like a human being, an English one from suburban south London, but in the meeting room he spoke as though he'd picked up his entire vocabulary from Business and Management manuals, and like his parents (nice people, mother a greengrocer, father a nurse, proud of him) were part of Chicago's criminal aristocracy.

Americans think British voices are darling. The British think American voices sing of potency and success. Acton was phoney through and through, but we didn't care. We relished the smoothness of his act. Estate agents aren't crooks, contrary to popular belief – I mean not many are – but we are all performers. We were accustomed to seeing each other, on heading out to meet a prospective buyer, pop on a new persona while picking up the keys. We knew, when Acton was bullshitting, that he was doing what he had to do, and the great thing was, if he succeeded, we each got a cut.

Diana had been surprised when he proposed that the entire sales department should pool their commissions. That wasn't normal, not in our outfit. She suspected that he was exploiting us, but he was subtler than that. He wanted us to love him more than we envied him. You couldn't imagine him getting his knees muddy, but he had a football coach's appreciation of group dynamics. When you think about it, team spirit isn't altruism. It just makes sense. One of the reasons he closed the most deals was that he kept the best properties for himself ('What my clients pay over-the-odds for is exclusivity,' he said), but another was that he was a brilliant salesman, seducer, beguiler, fiddler with the minds of the credulous. We all found him irritating: but we were all thankful for the luck of being on his team. It was down to him that I felt able to propose to Sophie that year, down to him that we got together the deposit for our flat in Harlesden. And, yes, it was Acton who spotted the flat in the first place and told me it was under-priced and that we should swoop. Sometimes a good leader lets a bit of profit pass, because to have your underlings indebted to you – that's gold.

Diana had known him since he was in nappies. He was her best friend's kid brother and the two girls, babysitting, would pootle around the bathroom while he watched them with a small boy's sly judgemental eyes. When they put on face-masks he cried. When they wiped them off again he chuckled, and danced a little foot-to-foot shuffle to celebrate their resumption of their normal selves. They made healthy carrot and hummus snacks for themselves – because they were teenaged girls and wanted to be clear-skinned and lovely – and he ate them. They cooked cocktail sausages and oven chips for him and – because they were teenaged girls and perpetually ravenous – they ate them faster than he could. They all dressed up together in his mother's clothes, the big girls prancing and preening in the mirror, with Prince playing, and the fat toddler tangling himself up in satin blouses that felt like cool water against his eczema. And then they shared hot water, getting in the bath together – little Acton propped and corralled by four skinny girl-legs, his eyes closed to savour the bliss of it, his eyes snapping open again to examine the sleek pale-and-rosy oddity of other people's flesh.

Diana told Sophie about those times once, when they met by chance at the gym. But she wouldn't have told me. She always plays by the rules. A senior manager does not invite a team member to imagine her in an informal domestic situation. Unprofessional.

Anyway that was all ages ago. When he applied for the job Diana left the decision to HR, and when he got it, unaided by her, she said, in front of all of us, 'I've known Acton for ever, but it doesn't necessarily follow that he'll be for ever in this job. As you'll all be able to tell him, what counts here isn't who knows who, it's who sells what.'

He sold. And he rose.

Hunting parties, he called them.

You'd have thought by that time there wouldn't have been any Victorian warehouses left undeveloped, but that just shows how wrong you can get. You had to go further out if you wanted affordable, naturally. But if money was no object there were still buildings whose owners had been playing a waiting game. There was one that came up in Wapping. Cinnamon Wharf. Acton was on it from the start. In fact he got it. And that's where the parties happened.

How did he get it? Like this.

We all ran. Everybody ran. From 12.30 to 2 p.m. the Embankment was a narrow arroyo with a stampede on. It looked like there'd been a fire in a city-sized gym, and men and women, grim-faced and sweating, were fleeing for their lives, with nothing on but lycra and nothing precious saved but their earbuds.

I'm a bit of an oenophile. In my daydreams professional men, wearing silk socks and silk ties and three pieces each of good suiting, treat each other to lunch – luncheon – in wood-panelled rooms where the meat comes round on trol-leys, and solicitous waiters press them to take a second Yorkshire pud or another ladleful of gravy with their bloody beef. That's the setting for the proper savouring of a good burgundy. That's the way our great-grandfathers did it. God knows how anyone got anything done in the afternoons. Now I drink my wine after work, by the glassful, standing up in a bar, with a sliver of *Comté* to complement it. The gratification of fleshly appetites during business hours is out. Lunchtime, like the rest of us, I'm out mortifying the flesh.

Acton ran too, but he didn't have a pedometer, or a thing-ummy on his phone that informed him how many calories he was consuming. Instead he had a map that he'd somehow got hold of (he had a friend in the planning department, every canny agent does) that showed him where buildings stood empty, where an application had been refused, where a free-holder was struggling to pay council tax. He'd sprint off in the right direction, nostrils aquiver, but once he was turning into the street he'd lollop along, laid-back, easy does it, a harmless young fellow with an interest in architecture, just keeping an eye out for a wrought-iron balustrade or fine tracery on a fanlight. Curious, yes, but not intrusive. Appreciative, not predatory. If there was somebody about he'd pause and hold his foot up to the back of his thigh, doing a bit of a stretch as anyone might, and ask some idle questions. Such unusual brickwork on that doorway. Bet that building's seen some things in its time. All converted into swanky studios now, probably? No? Owner must be pretty relaxed to let it stand empty. Oh. Sitting tenants? Poor guy.

And so he found Cinnamon Wharf.

Two hundred years ago that part of London was the end point of a journey from the other side of the earth. The merchants and ship-owners who lived in the handsome houses around Wapping Pier Head wanted pepper on their coddled eggs and nutmeg on their junket. Their daughters stuck cloves into oranges at Christmastime, in a neat tight knobbly pattern, and suspended the prickly balls in their closets, making their gowns aromatic. And what the merchants and their girls wanted, they reckoned others would want too, and would buy. The bales of sprigged calico and ivory-coloured muslin unloaded in Limehouse were scented by the spices that had travelled across the world alongside them in the hold. Prices were exorbitant, and fluctuated. With the arrival of every homing cargo they halved or, in the case of the more recherché cardamom, quartered. Shrewd traders stored sacks-full of the shrivelled seeds to await the next shortage and its advantageous effect on profit. By the time John Company ceded control of the spice-trade to the Queen-Empress's government the north shore of the Thames was walled, from Tower Bridge to Shadwell, by high buildings whose brick had blackened by the end of their first winter, and whose timbers were so imbued with the fragrant oils seeping out of the sacks that to walk along Wapping High Street was to imagine yourself in the southern oceans, where sailors used to navigate between islands by sniffing the perfumed breeze.

You see, we estate agents aren't all as weaselly and money-mad as we're cracked up to be. It's possible to feel the romance in London real-estate. And, so long as none of us ever lost sight of what we were there for, Diana was quite happy to hear us introduce a bit of history into our sales pitches. As long as the bathrooms and kitchen facilities were slap up to date, buyers could get quite excited about old-timey glamour.

Acton hung around and hung around and one day he was doing shoulder rotations outside the front door of the empty warehouse when a Bentley drew up, holly-green, so high off the ground there were fold-down steps for the passenger door. Headlights the shape of torpedo-heads mounted on the sides to add to its already prodigious width. Cream-coloured leather seats. Must have been seventy years old but looked box-fresh. The driver went round and opened the back door and a wizened little man got out. He needed the step.

He said, 'You can stop doing that. I know what you're after.'

Acton said, 'I'm delighted to meet you at last, Mr Rokesmith.' He'd done his research.

It all slotted into place. Acton put Rokesmith together with a contractor, and soon the Wharf had begun to smell, not of a Christmas-special latte, but of fresh plaster.

The flats were super-big. That was Acton's idea. He said, 'People buy a loft-style apartment because they want to pretend they're in downtown Manhattan with Jackson Pollock throwing paint around downstairs and Thelonius Monk jamming on the roof. They want places to party in. They want rusty iron beams and pockmarked floor-planks a foot wide. And what do they get? Bijoux little pods with wet rooms, because there's no room anywhere big enough for a bathtub. Places where you have to get on your hands and knees to look out of the window, because those idiot developers keep cramming in more floors. I tell you, Mr Rokesmith, if we can give them what they really want, you'll be a rich man.'

Rokesmith was amused. It was ages since he'd met anyone who'd pretend not to know that he was already about as rich as it was possible to be.

They sold the flats one or two at a time, always holding back the biggest one on the top floor. 'We'll make this the coolest address in town,' said Acton. 'They'll be tearing each other's fingernails out to get it.' Rokesmith didn't like that kind of talk. Violence was serious. Casual allusions to it offended him. Acton didn't always read him right.

He found him buyers though, the desirable kind. Single professionals. High net worth individuals. Metro-cosmopolitans. People whose job descriptions – consultant, content-provider, start-up strategist, marketing guru, director of comms – gave nothing away about what they actually did. A shop opened on Wapping High Street selling second-hand spectacle-frames in white Bakelite – the kind that golden-age Hollywood stars wore. You could have them made up to your own prescription, with photo-sensitive lenses. The greasy spoon turned into a cupcake café, and then a tapas bar, and finally settled down to being a gluten-free bakery. They started serving non-alcoholic pink prosecco in the pub. The bike-boys who arrived nightly at Cinnamon Wharf to deliver ready-meals featuring swordfish carpaccio and coriander-roasted salsify would pause if they saw Acton tapping in the security code, a couple of cool youngish people in black nylon jackets at his back, and give him a high-five.

I liked him, I really did. And not just because he cut me in on a bit of extra for the second-floor flats. I'm solid and he was flash. I like being shaken up a bit. People are always surprised when they meet Sophie. No one expects me to have a wife with teal-striped hair. What they don't get is that my winter tweeds and summer seersucker are fancy-dress too. Only in my case the artificial persona is Mr Trad. I polish my performance. I have a gift for dullness, for the fusty-musty. It has been useful to me, both professionally and in reconciling me to those aspects of my early life that I have no plans to revisit, not in conversation, not even alone and in silence in the long early-morning hours when I lie rigid, willing myself not to toss and turn. I have made myself into a lump of masonry – safe and sound and durable, no damp patches or shoddy construction. Having done so successfully, I enjoy being around gimcrack and glitter and trompe l'oeil.

*   *   *

So . . . the parties. Those Sunday nights. When the weekend's big push was done, there'd be trays of oysters delivered direct from Whitstable, and iced mint julep and vodka shots in gold-etched Moroccan glasses, all laid out in the empty penthouse at the top of Cinnamon Wharf. A dedicated lift went straight up there. You'd step out and, beyond the roof terrace's glass balustrade, the river's darkness would be all around, black water heaving almost imperceptibly, reflecting the hectic orange and magenta of a city at night.

Eliza came the first time. She was an excellent agent – proactive with sellers, confiding and cosy with buyers – but it's not always easy being the only woman on a team. I get that. On Tuesday morning (none of us customer-facing lot worked Mondays) she went into the glass box that was Acton's office, and pulled the blinds down as though what she had to say shouldn't be seen, let alone heard. After that she transferred to Lettings. Acton always treated her with the most perfect politeness. Behind her back though, especially when Diana was about, he referred more often than was really called for to the Manningtree Road debacle. Maybe Eliza missed a trick there, but I thought it was small-minded of him. It was ages ago and, anyway, let's face it, we all let slip an opportunity now and then.

By the time summer kicked in he'd stopped calling us his boys. He called us his dogs. Sundays, he'd invite clients, those he thought would be titillated by it – single men, the sort who wanted dimmer switches in the wet rooms. Mostly though, it was just us. 'I'm whistling up the pack,' he'd say to whoever was leaving the office with him.

To begin with, each time, it was all pretty raucous – everyone feeling that shiver as the pressure came off while the adrenalin was still way up there, and then the giddiness as the alcohol hit. Later, as the first of us started talking about the last train home, the atmosphere would shift and a different lot would be filtering in. Very young, all of them, very thin, female and male and some you couldn't be sure about. Their English was as uncertain as their immigration status, but they weren't there to make conversation.

I knew where they came from. Acton had helped them get access to an old gasworks in the Lea Valley. It was due for repurposing. He had his eye on it. Squatters were useful when you wanted to bring down an asking-price. And a few skinny junkies, once you'd given them the run of the en-suites in the unsold fourth-floor flat so that their hair smelt good again, and their piercings sparkled against pearly skin, lent quite a frisson to a party. The last-train lads stopped looking at their watches and by the time the dancing started the two packs were moving as one, spreading out on to the roof terrace. It looked as though you could dance off the edge and once the kids had started bringing out their pills and powders there were plenty of us there, on that airy dance floor, who weren't sure of the difference between down and up, between tiger-striped river-water and wine-dark sky.

It was an illusion of course. Perfectly solid breast-high panels of reinforced glass all around the roof's perimeter. Acton might play at being Dionysian but he wasn't about to risk a criminal negligence action. He had the greatest respect for the law of the land, as well as a thorough knowledge of the ways in which it could be circumvented. Besides, he was fully aware of what Rokesmith might do to him if he devalued the man's property by allowing some stray to die on it.

I don't believe he ever laid a finger with sexual intent on any of those hapless, gormless, spineless young things. What he liked was to observe what happened when the two breeds mingled. He'd step out onto the terrace, and sometimes I'd see him standing at ease by the sliding/folding doors – quiet, legs straddled, watching the dancers silhouetted against the luminous river. What was he hunting? Sex had something to do with it. Doesn't it always? But that wasn't really his primary interest. Power, I'd say.

One evening in September I was showing a couple of Russians around the river-view flat on the third floor at Cinnamon when I saw Eliza step out of the lift, look around like she'd got off at the wrong floor and get back into it. A week later, during a viewing with a client who liked to go house-hunting before breakfast, I saw her again in the lobby with someone I didn't know, hair scraped back, face shiny, wearing yoga pants. My client was going on to work. I was driving back to the office. I offered Eliza a lift.

I didn't ask. As far as I was concerned, Eliza could help herself to any set of keys that took her fancy, any time of the day or night. Subject to proper procedure. Provided she checked them out. Perhaps one of the purchasers was sub-letting. I wasn't sure what Rokers (as Acton had taken to calling the freeholder) would say to that, but it wasn't for me to interfere. It was she who seemed to feel she owed me some clarification. She jogged every morning from her flat in Limehouse, she said, and she liked to zip up to Cinnamon Wharf's roof for half an hour's meditation before taking a shower in the penthouse – we still weren't showing it – and walking on in to the office. Evenings, same thing in reverse.

'Did you know Eliza is up on the roof at Cinnamon most days?' I asked Acton in the wine bar a day or two later. We were celebrating the sale of the last of the fourth-floor flats. Acton liked a caipirinha. His drinking was probably a bit out of control but that wasn't my problem.

'Yeah,' he said. 'I've clocked her in the place a few times.' He didn't seem to want to take it any further, so we left it there.

Acton's partner William called me one day, and asked if we could talk. I liked him. He was gentle and patient. He lived pretty close – Acton had got him buying into the Kensal Rise golden triangle before it really took off – so we met on a Monday with our dogs in Tiverton Gardens. Sophie's dog, really, not mine. A graphic designer can carry a photogenic spaniel into work with her. An estate agent not so much: dog hair on a suit doesn't look good. Anyway, our flossy little beast was running round in large circles with William's French bulldog when he began to cry. He hadn't seen Acton for a month he said. He just wanted to know, was he all right?

People think, because I'm kind of passive socially, that I'm observant and considerate and wise. This isn't true. I really don't care much about other people's emotional lives. I'd had no idea they'd broken up.

'Six weeks ago,' he said. 'And frankly it doesn't make much difference. He hadn't really spoken to me for nearly a year. I mean talking yes, but not really to me. Like I existed. You know?'

I said something fatuous about going through a bad patch.

'No,' he said. 'It's over. But I wanted to know if he was all right. It got so weird. The way he started to stare at me all the time.'

'Staring. Like how?'

'Well, he was entitled, wasn't he. Lovers are allowed to look at each other. He saw me naked all the time. So I don't know why it freaked me out. Watching my mouth while I was eating. Watching my arse when I was bent over the dishwasher. Watching my hands when I was ironing. Too interested. There were a few times I was taking a shower and when I'd finished I'd see him there in the bathroom, like he'd sprung from nowhere, and I'm telling you that is one small bathroom. Just standing there. If he'd been waiting to drag me back to bed – no problem. But we didn't do much of that, the last few months. His choice, not mine.'

I thought of Acton on the roof, watching a load of mismatched couples with their hands all over each other. I thought of the way, in the office, his eyes followed Diana around.

Here is Acton's idea of a party. Oysters, cocktails – yeah yeah yeah. All that. Dancing, naturally – he had a serious pair of speakers. Mac'n'cheese, coming up hot and ready, a jaunty little red-and-white striped trolley trundling out of the lift wheeled by an enormous man whose employer had made enough from party-catering to buy Flat 2 on Floor 3. We ate it from brown cardboard boxes with wooden forks. No plastic

– the firm sponsored all sorts of enviro-friendly eco-housing ventures. 'What for?' I asked Diana. She looked blank. 'The built environment,' she said, 'and the natural environment are partners, not rivals.' No flicker of irony. She must have forgotten about . . . well . . . things we'd all decided not to talk about any more. Not until someone called us out on them.

Diana didn't come to the hunting parties. That would have been unthinkable. Diana is the soul of rectitude. She doesn't do silly.

More dancing. Karaoke. Those faun-like waifs drifting through the crowd like they were weightless. One or other of us boys catching one of them, like closing your hand on a will-o'-the-wisp. Couples slinking off into corners. The music dimming. People flat on their backs on the terrace's decking, heads resting on each other's shoulders and bellies, telling each other their self-pitying little life stories, or reminiscing about deals they'd done together, or just talking the kind of rubbish that made their bodies shake with laughter until everyone was linked in a communion of shared mirth, and that's about the time it would become seriously Actonian. Because Acton's were the only parties I'd ever been to where everyone, every time, ended up sitting in a circle like a pack of cubs. Not the boy-scouty kind of cubs. We weren't tying knots or memorising Morse code. We were watching those damaged young people, entwined in a kind of circlet of bone-white flesh. And in the centre Acton, fully clad, his thighs straining the cloth of his silky Armani trousers as he sat with his knees up, corralled by skinny limbs, his round eyes (without his specs they looked even rounder) watching us watching the kids and watching Acton watching.

Did I say he was hunting for power? I'm wrong. It was far more complicated than that.

I have two tableaux I keep stacked away at the back of my mind. One dates from my childhood, and I'm not taking it out to look at it again now. Put away childish things. There's a hand down some trousers, and a nauseating smell and a voice saying, 'Keep going. Keep going. There's nothing to worry about, boy. I've got my eye on you.' The other scene is set in the penthouse and it's a lot pleasanter to contemplate. I'm with a gaggle of nymphets, three gawky Bambis with dark eyes and fluttery hands. It's true the one with her head in my lap seemed to be crying, but they were a snivelly lot. I didn't see the harm.

If it had been up to Eliza, it's unlikely there would have been any kind of stink. She is a very self-contained and self-reliant person and I believe she would have dealt with the issue discreetly. She'd told me once, when another agent got their dirty little mitts on a prime site with planning permission that we should have had exclusive, 'Not for me to butt in but, just saying . . . The only way to keep a secret is not to tell people. Not to tell anyone. You boasted about it, didn't you, to some friend of yours who's got nothing to do with the biz, so you thought it was safe?'

It was true. I had.

'Remember,' she said. 'No one.'

So when she noticed the way Acton was hanging around she kept quiet, but one morning, when they were in the penthouse, her personal trainer saw that Acton was out on the roof terrace. Seeing. And Eliza didn't say 'Keep your mouth shut' because that would only have aggravated the thing. And the personal trainer mentioned it to Diana, and that was that.

> *'One's not quite enough.*
> *Two leaves you wanting more.*
> *Three is a disaster.*
> *Acton's on the floor.'*

He'd had his three caipirinhas but he was still upright, chanting that doggerel in the bar we all frequented. I took his arm and got him into the backroom where I'd been sampling a Chablis with a solicitor who shared my interests. Griddled scallops to go with. She was an attractive female solicitor, but there was no need for Sophie to know that. Anyway, she pissed off home as soon as Acton started hollering.

'Get a grip,' I said.

'What's to grip?' he said, subdued now, maudlin. 'I've got nothing to grip onto. I'm lost. All those bitches are coming after me now. View halloo. Tally ho. With super-bitch leading the pack.'

Diana? Eliza?

All or any of them. Acton's self-pity had transformed all women into bloodhounds.

'And which of you rotten curs is going to help me?'

I took him home. William was waiting by the door. I'd called him. 'I don't have a key any more,' he said, 'but if he needs me . . .' We had to wrestle Acton's key ring from him while he babbled out his grievances against the ungrateful world. William lifted him over the threshold and begun shushing him as a parent shushes a wailing brat.

So what had happened? There are, as there always are, several ways of understanding the story. All the variants added up to one thing. Acton had been where he should not have been. He had seen what he should not have seen.

Bluff no-nonsense version . . . Woman, imagining herself alone in an empty flat (except for personal trainer of course), takes shower. Man happens by and sees what he shouldn't. Blushes all round. No harm done.

But it's not quite that simple. For one thing, Eliza wasn't alone in the shower. For another, she and the personal trainer had both seen Acton loitering on the roof terrace a couple of times before, around the time they came back from their evening run, so perhaps happenstance didn't have that much to do with his being there.

Other versions were broadcast around the office in a babble of whispers.

'William says they haven't done it for, like, years.'

'I mean it's not a crime to like watching.'

'Sex clubs, you have a whole room full of people, don't you?'

'That's different. That's consensual.'

There was the lubricious version: 'I wouldn't have minded an eyeful of that.' The righteously indignant: 'We owe it to all our female clients . . .' The sheepish: 'Well, come on – we've all had some fun up there.' The collusive: 'Best not rock the boat. I mean, good old Acton . . .' The prurient: 'What do you mean, on her knees?' The legalistic: 'Strictly speaking, they were all in breach of our agreement with Rokesmith.' There were many variations on the creeped-out version. For everyone, suddenly, the picture of Acton, gloating over the entangled fauns, had ceased to be funny. And then there was the abject, frankly scared-shitless-of-losing-our-jobs afraid: 'We have to tell Diana, don't we? I mean if she hears and nobody's spoken up . . .'

And then came the twist, 'Haven't you heard? Diana *knows*. Diana was *there*.'

There. Where? In the shower too? How? What doing? How positioned? On her knees?

To start with I imagined the trainer as one of those small-skulled, tremendously muscled, encouraging young men you see moving their clients' limbs around in a physiotherapeutic kind of way in the park on a Sunday. When someone said, 'No no, Doris is all-woman,' the story's significance suddenly switched. To watch a lusty woman having it off with an ideal embodiment of masculinity – that's one thing. That's to be a boy cheering on another boy at play. But to trespass into a women-only get-together, that's different. That's a no-no. That's sweet poison. Imagine it. Three women. My mind swerves away.

William texted me: 'Can we meet?' When we did, he said, 'I want you to know that Acton wasn't a voyeur. Not that kind of a one anyway. I don't think he ever even looked at porn. He didn't want to watch sex. He just liked looking at bodies. At my feet, my hands, my elbows, the dip in my back, the way my neck meets my shoulders. He liked the look of naked flesh, that's all.'

He seemed very agitated. It mattered to him that I understood. But to me peeping is peeping. I respected Diana. If she and Eliza, or she and the trainer, or all three together, were having it away, or not, that was their business. That wasn't the point. The transgression was Acton's.

One of the first things I learnt as a child was not-seeing. Shut your eyes and count to twenty. Shut your eyes and hold out your hands. Shut your eyes while Daddy's undressing. Shut your eyes while I just . . . Don't look until I tell you. Nothing to worry about. I'm just . . . Don't look.

As I said, there are things from which I have chosen to avert my eyes, though they are – in a very profound and distressing sense – my own. Promiscuous looking – idly curious, lubricious, or simply appreciative – I see it as a pernicious liberty to take.

Diana called us in one by one. We were all intimidated by her, but we didn't fully have her measure. We mistook her reserve for uptightness. She didn't muck in, so we tended to ignore her, deferring instead to her chosen deputies, Acton among them. We hadn't really understood how she'd run us. Now she showed her power.

She handed us teeth. She stroked our fingers until the claws grew. She stiffened our jaws until they clenched like pliers. She lengthened our spines and hardened our skulls and made our eyes into laser guns and our noses into missiles. She growled at us until we growled back, maddened by our own subservience. She let it be known that we were her pack now, and there was to be no mercy for mavericks. She invoked Rokesmith and the likely consequences of his displeasure – should anything go wrong in that direction – for our end-of-year bonuses. I squirmed and whined. I'm not proud of the way I behaved that week, the tales I bore to Diana as though they were duck she'd shot down and I was her retriever, the confidences I betrayed, the mean little niggling ways in which I tried to tell her that it was her hand I wanted fondling my ears and rubbing my tummy when I'd pleased her, that it would be her voice I obeyed when it told me to go fetch.

She said that Rokesmith had found a buyer for the penthouse. 'Thanks to Eliza,' she said. 'Yes, she's back in Sales. She'll be heading up the team from next week.' We got the picture.

Acton didn't come in on Tuesday or Wednesday or Thursday, but Friday he was there again. 'There'll be one last party,' said Diana. 'In the penthouse. Before completion. Tomorrow in fact.' When Rokesmith wanted something done, the lawyers got a move on.

Diana wasn't there herself. She didn't work weekends. Saturdays, she was in Richmond Park with her other hounds. She didn't need to be present in person. She'd trained and instructed and starved us, and she'd showed us the lure with Acton's scent on it.

It began with teasing. Acton was very smartly turned out. He wore one of those tight-buttoned shortish jackets that set off the amplitude of a man's backside. All the better to sink your teeth into.

We all knew that one of the kids had been found dead in the gasworks. Overdose. You could have seen it coming. No one's fault but her own, but still . . . We made jokes about gas masks and gaslight and gas chambers. They weren't funny jokes. They weren't meant to be. Acton laughed anyway. He was full of bonhomie. He could always turn it on.

He was onto the third caipirinha when he sensed the shift. He said something disparaging about a client, one we'd all had to deal with, one of those time-wasters whose idea of Saturday-morning fun is to go sightseeing around property way out of their price range. We didn't laugh. It wasn't that we liked the woman – she treated us all like she'd learnt at her mother's knee that all estate agents are dishonest spivs whose vocabulary is risibly limited to words like 'comprising' and 'utility room'. It wasn't because we'd never jeered at her ourselves that we denied him his laugh. We kept quiet because we were all pointing, every sinew tight, each right-side forefoot lifted ready and each muzzle trained on the chosen prey.

Acton put his drink down and his eyes swivelled a bit. He struggled on with his anecdote. He mentioned a shower attachment. He uttered the words en suite. It was as though it was a code word, a command like Attaboy or Rats. Beneath our summer-weight jackets our hackles rose. We crowded him. We barged and jostled. We made a half-circle with Acton as Piggy-in-the-Middle, hemmed in, with the glass panels behind him, and behind them nothing but the purple air.

*   *   *

Mr Rokesmith seemed to rather relish the media coverage of Acton's plummet, and of the party preceding it. An orgy, they called it, which was absurd. It's not as though anyone's clothes were off. 'No harm done,' said Rokesmith, 'apart from the demise of your young friend. Sorry about that. Smart fellow.'

The sale went ahead. Contracts had been exchanged, after all. People who want to live on that stretch of river like to be reminded of the East End of their imagination, of opium dens and mutilated prostitutes and Ronnie Kray saying, 'Have a word with the gentleman outside, would you, Reg?' If you want Kensington, you know where to find it. But Wapping, well, it's got a bit of a frisson, hasn't it? Even if rowdiness at an estate agents' office party doesn't quite cut it in the glamour-of-evil stakes.

Diana assured the police we were all exemplary beings – docile, obedient, team-spirited. We weren't charged with anything. We were good boys. We got our bonuses.

She still calls us her pack. We are still let out for exercise at lunchtime. We run together along the Embankment. Our muscles work fluidly beneath our elastic skins. We keep our heads low and our weight well forward. The little gizmos slung around our necks allow her to find us swiftly should we stray.

Our eyes switch sideways to check each other's proximity – we don't like to be isolated. We know the hindermost and the leader are both easy prey. Acton was our leader once. Look what happened to him.

PSYCHE

There was once a young woman whom no one wanted to touch. It's not that she was ugly. No. The problem was that she was too beautiful by far.

Her skin was as smooth and matt as crêpe de Chine. You wouldn't want to stroke her cheek for fear of rumpling it. Her hair was as lustrous as falling water and as black as squid ink. If you ran your fingers through it – or so the young men thought as they watched her walking to the library – you'd be afraid they'd come away coated in darkness or cut as by a million tiny wires.

She walked always with her shoulders back. Her hips swayed around the invisible plumb line which dropped from the crown of her head. Her centre of gravity was high, but securely poised. You couldn't really picture yourself tumbling onto a mattress, giggling, with a girl like that.

You couldn't see yourself kissing her, either, or blowing raspberries on her naked belly, or sucking her toes.

She was called Psyche.

Her parents were proud of her, but not as pleased as they supposed they ought to be. Their friends said, 'You know what they're like. I never know how many I'm cooking for.' They said, 'I haven't seen him for days, hardly. He's always in his room with that creepy friend of his. I've no idea what they do up there.' They said, 'She's dyslexic.' 'He's dyspraxic.' 'She's anorexic.' 'We've tried counselling.' They said, 'I think they should do their own washing, don't you? But you know. Sometimes, the smell . . .' They said, 'You've got to let them do it their own way, haven't you?'

Psyche's parents kept quiet. They really had nothing to complain about. Sometimes, at night, though, one of them would say, 'Do you think Psyche's all right? I mean, really?' and the other would look out of the window, or pick a towel up off the floor, or neatly square off a pile of books, and then say, 'Well, we've no reason to suppose that she isn't, have we?'

They hadn't. No reason at all. There was nothing wrong with Psyche. She was no trouble. It was just a bit funny the way that she had no friends.

The boys of the town were offended. They didn't like a young woman to be so negligent of them. They swaggered about, these boys, their hair falling forward over their eyes, their tight trousers puckering around their ankles. Their boots were scuffed. Silver studs gleamed in their nostrils and gold hoops in their ears. They looked like desperadoes, but they were very easily upset.

The war memorial was their place. In the mornings they'd stand around it. They turned their collars up and smoked. Or they sat on the steps and ate bacon sandwiches, holding them carefully with both hands so that the brown sauce wouldn't run out. They'd talk chorically, each one addressing all the others, each one adding a detail to the story they were telling themselves, mumbling, catching no one's eye, with occasional barks of laughter. Then they'd scatter, to do whatever they each did by day, and when it was nearly dark they'd be back, waiting for the story to progress, waiting for the night's episode to unfold.

Psyche saw them when she came out of the library. She said hello, pleasantly, to the ones she'd known at school, and walked on by.

The other young women passed in pairs or gaggles. They went noisily away up the side streets to shop for lip-balm or tights, or they settled in flocks around the tin tables outside the bar. They sat on each other's laps when the chairs were all taken, and shared each other's drinks – three, four, five straws converging in tall glasses full of ice-cubes and sliced fruit. They looked at the boys. The boys kept talking, and fiddled with their cigarette lighters. After a while one – the one whose leather jacket looked old and soft, its blackness whitened by scars – walked over to two girls coming back into the square with carrier bags, and he put his arm across the tall one's shoulders, and her friend took her carrier bags without being asked, and the tall girl and the boy went away towards the river. That was the beginning of the night.

Psyche was at home. She had supper with her parents and her sister and her sister's fiancé. They ate fish pie with broccoli. Then she went up to her room. She sat in the rocking chair that her mother had sat in to nurse her when she was a baby and, because she had been reading all day and needed to use another part of her mind, she put on her headphones so as not to disturb anyone and listened to a couple of Bach partitas while she did some petit point.

A boy called Crispin said, 'That girl who comes out of the library every time? The one with the black hair? Where does she go off to?'

The boy he'd asked said, 'Fuck her. Who cares? Who's bothered? Who needs her?'

Crispin said, 'I just wondered, is all.' He went home early that night. It felt a bit boring in the square.

When Psyche's sister got married the boys all got together in a corner of the marquee and made a plan. They were uncomfortable in their hired or borrowed suits but each one of them secretly thought he looked pretty sharp. None of them wanted to get married, not for a long while, but there's something about a wedding. Not just the booze. The bride in all that lace and filmy stuff, the groom looking solemn, the kissing. It's just weird, one of them said. All these aunts and uncles and the teacher from primary school and Psyche's sister's boss and her husband who was in the police force – they'd all come to celebrate two people getting it on. It was so blatant, so embarrassing. The air quavered and pulsed with eroticism. Even the little bridesmaids were flushed and jumpy. It put the boys on edge.

Psyche wasn't a bridesmaid. She'd said thank you, what an honour, but if her sister didn't mind she'd rather be in the pew with the rest of the family, and that way she could make sure Granny was all right, and wouldn't it be sweet if the bridal procession was all made up of their pretty little cousins.

Secretly, her sister was relieved. She'd been thinking pearl-grey for Psyche, but she knew that even if you wrapped her up in fog she would still dominate the picture.

Crispin had a cousin who was an embarrassment to him. Mackeson, he was called. He didn't talk much. From a distance Mackeson looked superb – tall, broad-shouldered, narrow-hipped, a sculpted totem of virility. When you came close though, you could smell his breath and see how his irises slid around in their yellow whites. When he was younger he used to wait under the holly bush by the jink in the road near the old chapel and if a woman came by on her own he'd jump out and grab her breasts and twist them. He stopped doing that after he was beaten up by Iris the baker's girl's brothers. Now he worked in the garage. Most of the young women of the town knew to stay away from him. Sometimes, at night, people in the house where he had a basement room would hear his muttering punctuated by a hoarse, retching groan.

Mackeson was at the wedding, his thick hair slicked down, in a decent grey suit. His biceps distorted the shape of the sleeves so that they rode up and looked too short for him. His hands, which were large and pale, were frightening to see. Because he was a bit older, too old to have been at school with her, and because she never listened to gossip, Psyche didn't know about him. She saw that he was standing alone and when he stared at her she went up to him kindly and asked him was he a friend of the groom's? That's when the boys made their plan.

They wouldn't have to tell Mackeson what he was to do. Rape came naturally to him. They just needed to provide an opportunity.

Afterwards they all felt ashamed of themselves. They weren't bad boys, and not one of them had ever forced himself on a girl. Not really. Sometimes you couldn't be sure whether they wanted it or not. But not really. Not forced as such. It was all a kind of joke. The thing was that Psyche was so serious about everything. For fuck's sake, couldn't she see it was a joke?

Crispin wasn't told about the plan. That was crucial.

One day, in the week following the wedding, Crispin wasn't at the war memorial, not in the evening when everyone else was there. He'd been in the square earlier, at lunchtime. He worked weekends at the hospital, so he got Thursdays off. He sat on the steps by himself from eleven thirty until three. There were some kids around, bare-kneed boys who should surely have been in school. They were kicking about under the plane-trees. People having lunch in the café looked at Crispin curiously but there was nothing remarkable to see apart from the cleanness of his white shirt and the quickness of his hands as they flickered over his travelling chess set. He waited, and he sang to himself. At three he thought she's not coming out, and he went into the library, and there was Psyche, wearing glasses, and although he'd known perfectly well he'd see her there he was shocked by the joy her presence brought him.

He went up and sat sideways on the edge of her desk, and fiddled with a stapler, while the chief librarian looked quizzically at him.

'I was waiting outside,' he said. 'I thought we might have gone for a walk on your break.' Psyche made a little shooing movement with her hands and he stood up properly and faced her.

The chief librarian said, 'Psyche didn't take a break today. We're re-shelving Biography D to F and we thought if we stopped we'd get confused.' He was a kind man and he worried about Psyche's dedication to her work almost as much as he welcomed and exploited it. He said, 'I brought in flapjack so we wouldn't starve. But even so . . .' He said, 'Why don't you take that walk now, Psyche? You're owed a couple of hours off, after all.'

The summer was nearly over and the light flew horizontally, lighting up the undersides of the pigeons swooping over the square. Mauve, rose-pink and cloudy greys. When Crispin looked at Psyche the low sun was in his eyes and there were rainbows in his lashes and all he saw of her was a kind of glory. When Psyche looked at him she saw curls and curves. She saw skin pale and blue-shaded as mother-of-pearl, and a mouth as red and sensitive as a sea-anemone. She smelt Knight's Castile soap, the kind her father used, a smell that that was neither feminine nor medicinal, that was simply the scent of cleanliness. She knew he was besotted with her. The signs were familiar. Sometimes her suitors annoyed her. Sometimes she was afraid of them. But this time she felt only a wistful tenderness. He looked so young!

What Crispin didn't know was that he was bait. The schoolboys who'd been mooching around in the square were lookouts. They had been posted there by their big brothers. They took it in turns to drop into the barber's shop where one of the big brothers worked, to report developments. He's still just sitting there – what a loser. Still there. Still there. He's eating an apple. He's playing a board game all by himself. Still there. He's gone into the library – about fucking time. He's come out with that girl, the long-haired one. They're buying chips. They're going towards the river. They're leaning against the wall. They're still just standing there. He's hopping around and doing all the talking and she's just looking at him. No. They're off. They're going towards the bridge. They're under the bridge.

Under the bridge, the footpath dwindled to a slimy ledge with only a rusted iron railing to save one from slipping. It was noisy there, the river compressed into a narrow channel and its roar echoing off the black brick vaults. Psyche thought it was marvellous that the bridge-builders had been as careful of the grandeur of this underspace as they were of the handsome stone parapet above. Psyche appreciated scrupulous workmanship. She responded to symmetry. She sometimes thought of training as an engineer. She scarcely noticed the schoolboy whistling a signal behind them. It was at least six seconds after Crispin had spotted them, with dread, that she noticed the three people who had appeared, as though from nowhere, on the narrow walkway ahead.

Crispin pushed gallantly ahead to protect her. He couldn't tell for certain, because of the darkness down there, and the balaclavas, who they were, but he could make a pretty good guess. When he smelt the breath of the one who tripped him and slid him into the water, he knew it was Mackeson. As the river tumbled him away he saw the other two yank Psyche off her feet and then hoick her up, one taking her legs and the other her arms, and carry her at a run into the side-tunnel that led along secret passageways to – what? Nobody knew, because when they were little the local children were too scared to explore, and by the time they were bigger they no longer cared.

Psyche wasn't calm exactly, but she was surprised to find that the mind can keep coming up with ideas and observations even in situations of bewilderment and peril. She had seen Crispin borne away, so there was no point shouting for him. Suspended as she was she couldn't do anything to save herself. She could speak though, so she asked the obvious questions – what are you doing where are you taking me who are you anyway why – not so much because she expected answers as because speech is orderly and rational and might help to counter the violence that had broken over her tidy life.

The river ran through the town walled in by embankments. Crispin let it take him. He knew where a car had crashed through the railing years ago. His mother had taken him along in his pushchair to see the extraordinary sight of it lying belly-up in the water with all its dirty black workings exposed – the first time he could remember that he'd ever been out of the house after dark. He'd cried when he saw it because it reminded him of the time he'd put his tortoise on the coffee table to feed it and the silly armoured thing had walked off the edge and cracked its shell on the tiles and had to be stuck together again with glue. It wasn't until years later that his mother had said to him, taunting, 'You going on about that tortoise when there was a woman drowned there right in front of you!' He hadn't had a clue. Anyway, he wasn't going to forget where the wreck was and he was ready to kick like mad to avoid being scraped over its jagged metal. Otherwise he waited. He kept his strength for when the river broadened and he could splash ashore and run full pelt back to wherever it was Psyche had been taken.

They met him as he came panting up the incline towards the bridge. Three boys, his friends. They said, 'They locked her in the pump-room with Mackeson.' Crispin tried to push past them but they held him by his arms. 'It's been half an hour,' they said. 'No point trying to save her now. You'll get slaughtered.' He was frantic. He struggled, but he was exhausted. His clothes were sopping wet and the blood thundered so behind his forehead he couldn't really grasp what they were saying. The biggest one hugged him, and he sobbed.

Mackeson appeared at the other end of the bridge, walking up the steps from the towpath, holding onto the green-painted wrought-iron railing and hauling himself up. He looked at them, looked quickly away and shuffled off. Crispin writhed out of his friends' grip and went after him, and the other boys let him go. Mackeson was his cousin, after all.

Crispin grabbed Mackeson's donkey jacket and tried to turn him round to get a look at his face, but Mackeson didn't slow down. He pressed on, hands in pockets. Crispin let go and dashed ahead and got in his way so that their eyes met. Mackeson didn't look like a triumphant violator of young women. He was flushed and snotty and mumbling. Suddenly he dragged Crispin down a side street, and rammed him up against a wall, and said, 'You've got to go to her.'

Crispin was furious. He said, 'What have you done?'

Mackeson said, 'I couldn't. I couldn't. They gave me a torch so I could see her. They said to do it but she just lay there looking at me. I don't like girls looking at me. You know her. Just go down there. Get her out of there. I left the gate open.'

'She'll think I knew. She'll think I took her there on purpose.'

'Go on,' said Mackeson.

Crispin went. He ran along the towpath, his feet silent in canvas shoes. He saw the other boys coming out of the tunnel and walking off the other way. He plastered himself to the wall until they were gone. He went slowly into the blackness. He brought out his lighter and by its tiny gleam he found the barred gate across the round entranceway like the mouth of a cave, and he pushed against it and was in.

He groped around until he felt the warm smoothness of Psyche's hair. He gasped and flinched back. She said very calmly, 'Which one are you?' He didn't answer. He knelt down, She was sitting on a kind of bench. She said, 'Poor Mackeson. Why do you bully him so?' Crispin laid his head on her lap. Still he didn't dare speak. He couldn't bear that she should ever know that it was him, that she should ever know that he was there, even though it really hadn't been his fault at all.

She put her hand very lightly on his head. She knew him by his curls. She smiled in the dark. His clothes were sopping wet. She didn't know how it had all happened, but she knew she didn't need to be afraid of him.

She kept her hand on his head and gradually he stilled like a nervous animal soothed by stroking.

She said, 'I'm going to leave now. Don't follow me. I'm going to walk home through the middle of town. I'll come back tomorrow after supper.' She stood up and hit her head on the vaulted ceiling and said drat, and found her way to the gate, and took the key, with a scraping and a jangling, so no one could lock it again, and walked away toward the dim glimmer of daylight where the tunnel came out under the bridge. Crispin heard the firm even sound her low-heeled shoes made on the paving stones.

When she got home her mother said, 'There's a damp patch on your good skirt. The flowers must have been dripping.' Psyche had stopped in the square and bought a bunch of chrysanthemums for her parents because it was their wedding anniversary. She was such a thoughtful daughter.

They met again in that lightless chamber the following evening, and the one after that, and the one after that, and so on through most of the winter. No one disturbed them. The other boys didn't come back. They didn't want to think about their prank. It hadn't been any fun, with Mackeson getting the wind up like that, and now when they saw Psyche they tried to kid themselves that she might have forgotten all about it. As though that was likely. As though a person's getting dragged off into the underworld and all-but-raped was a common occurrence.

Psyche hadn't forgotten, and never would, but she wasn't frightened and she wasn't angry. She was a bit surprised it had happened to her, because she had noticed, from nursery school upward, that the victims of bullying had something pregnable about them. Their personalities had cracks in them, into which an ill-intentioned person could insert a pointed stick. She didn't think she was like that. But then, she reflected, she had changed that afternoon. When she leant against the low wall along the riverbank while Crispin kept babbling on, telling her stories and watching her sideways to check whether he was making her laugh, she had felt herself changing. Perhaps that was why.

The other thing that surprised her was that – and she truly believed this, incredible as it seemed – Crispin didn't know that she knew that it was he who came evening after evening, and took her in his arms in the cave.

The cave was cosy now. It was dry as could be. When Psyche came, the day after the outrage, the hard stone bench, which was really a kind of storage space for firewood, was hard no longer. Someone – Crispin obviously – had brought quilts and cushions. And another day there was a blanket to cover them and a little later there was a fur rug, which must have been real fur because at one end of it there was a tail, and at the other a snarling muzzle, with teeth, which lay beside their heads like a benevolent guard-dog, protecting their privacy as they ran their hands over each other's smooth skin in the pitch-darkness, and ran their tongues around the inside of each other's soft mouths.

Crispin never spoke, because he fancied himself unknown. Psyche spoke unguardedly, as she had never spoken before. She told her silent and invisible friend about pleasure, and self-abandonment, and the reckless luxury of mindlessness. He listened, and felt, naturally enough, rather smug, for was it not he who was conferring on her all this bliss? And vice versa, of course, but he preferred to think of himself as the conferrer, and that suited Psyche too, because all day every day she was considerate and responsible, and it was a treat for her to feel greedy in the darkness of the cave where she could grind her teeth as the moment of ecstasy approached and screw up her eyes and generally conduct herself in a way which would have been positively unseemly had there been anyone there who could see.

One day she said, 'I wonder where you got this tiger-skin, or whatever it is?' Another day she said, 'It's wonderful how you change the pillowcases and bring flowers so this place always smells fresh.' Another day she said, 'Dried apricots! How is it you always choose my favourite things? It's as though our minds speak to each other without words.' And on each occasion Crispin was puzzled. He hadn't brought any pillowcases or bearskins or candied fruit. Surely it must have been Psyche who did so. He didn't quite get what game she was playing, but he curled himself into her back and crossed his hands over her breasts and blew, gently, gently, on the back of her neck until she was sighing and turning towards him and lacing her long clever fingers in his give-away curly hair. Sometimes in the absolute darkness they lost their sense of direction, and it was as though up and down were no longer opposite, and in the apricot-perfumed globe that was their pleasure-dome they flew, cartwheeling together as warm and safe and contentedly sightless as unborn baby twins.

'She seems different somehow,' said Psyche's mother.

'I wonder where she goes after supper,' said her father, and the two of them looked at each other as though they shared a naughty secret. But actually they hadn't a clue what was happening to Psyche. When she came in, in good time for supper (she didn't cook – she did the drying up afterwards), they said things about the sunset (lurid) or the upcoming election (worrying) or Granny (you can't blame her, poor old thing). Sometimes one of them said, 'Do you still see anything of Jemima?' – Jemima had a very eligible brother. Or they said, 'Jerry's mother says he and all his mates go to the ice-rink all the time – it's quite a craze.' Or they said, 'I expect there's a lot of extra work to be done at the library for this centenary thing.' Or they said, 'You know, Precious, you can always invite your friends back here for supper. Any time you like. Really.'

Psyche smiled and said yes, or gosh, or not really, and once she'd finished the putting-away she'd pick up her coat and say, 'I won't be late.' And she wasn't late, not very, but when she came in and took her shoes off, so as not to disturb them or track mud up the stair carpet, a breeze stirred through the house, warm and vivacious and redolent of new-sprung grass.

One day Psyche met Mackeson in the street. It was, after all, a very small town. He was aghast. He tried to make himself inconspicuous, but that was never going to work. He had given up shaving. By the smell of it, he'd given up washing too. The little children ran behind him shouting. They called him Monsterson. Psyche didn't hesitate. She went up to him and held out her hand so resolutely that he had to take it. She said, 'I know you never meant me any harm. You're their slave, aren't you, slave to those other boys. They use you as though you were a big frightening dog.'

The boys had wanted Mackeson to fall for her in his usual gross and lustful way. That hadn't happened. He had recoiled as a horse might jib if asked to mount a swan. But when she was kind to him he was immediately her swain. He wanted to give her whatever he could. All he had to offer was a piece of information. He said, 'You know it's Crispin who meets you in the pump-room every night, don't you?'

'Yes,' she said, 'I know.'

Then he said, 'But do you know the other thing about Crispin?'

Psyche was curious. There were many things to be said about Crispin, about how fragile he seemed, and how strong, about how his deep voice seemed older than the boyish mouth it issued from (how she wished he would speak to her), about those curls, and yes, she knew now that the hairs on his thighs grew like tight little springs as well. She wondered which thing it was that Mackeson wanted to tell her about. She felt she needed all the information she could get because she realised that her pretending not to recognise Crispin, that had seemed at first like a game, had become a trap, and sooner or later – probably very soon – it would close on them. It would be embarrassing. Neither of them would be able to explain the deceptions they'd been practising. Crispin would feel humiliated or betrayed. She said, 'No, I don't. Tell me.'

Then Mackeson went down on one knee. He actually did. He wasn't offering her a ring, or wedlock. He had to kneel because he was so tall, and he wanted to whisper. The words slid clammily into Psyche's ear.

They surprised her profoundly. She said, 'I don't believe you.'

He said, 'I can't help that. It's true.'

'I'll ask him,' she said.

'He'll be upset. He'll guess I told you. Please don't.'

'Sometimes,' she said slowly, 'he falls asleep after we've . . . I could look at him then.'

* * *

And so it all fell out as it always does in this story. The boy who was all made of love, whose whole identity was made up of his loveliness, his lovability, his lovingness, was exposed to the scrutiny of an enquiring and appraising mind. It wasn't a drop of heated oil that Psyche let drop onto her sleeping lover's white shoulder; it was the still smouldering tip of the match she had struck to pry into his nature. He woke. He fled.

Sometimes the story continues. Sometimes Psyche is punished by Love for her lack of trust, but, after many trials, she is found fit to be reunited with the curly-haired conferrer of bliss. But this time I don't think that is going to happen. I think Psyche will marry the chief librarian, with whom she has a lot in common. Her career will prosper. She'll be promoted over his head and, being an unambitious man, he'll not resent it. Her parents will tell each other how pleased they are that she's settled down, but they'll remember those nights when a perfumed breeze filled their decent terraced house with voluptuous promises and – separately, secretly – each of them will grieve for what their sensible girl has lost.

And Mackeson will always be Psyche's devoted follower. And she will recommend a dentist for him, and he will recover his self-respect in her service, and he will lose his shifty look and eventually his physical splendour will be unveiled so strikingly that she will take to meeting him, when the librarian is working late, in the pump-room down the tunnel beneath the bridge. They will couple in darkness, which Mackeson prefers, because the way women look at him upsets him, but Psyche will always derive satisfaction from watching his superb figure moving around the town and knowing he is hers.

Crispin – well I can't say exactly what happens to Crispin, but wherever he chooses to lie down there will always be clean pillowcases, and the furry pelt of a wild animal, and the scent of apricots, and usually some girl.

PASIPHAE

Minos paid his people on a Friday, late afternoon, just like any other employer. His business was different from most, though. His crew weren't knocking off for the weekend. They were getting started. He liked them to be flush when they were selling. He wanted them to have that swagger, to be the people other people liked to be around. The other unusual thing was that every week Minos offered to play them double or quits for their pay. It wasn't compulsory. Lots of the women refused and he let it go. Paid them straight. Cash in hand. The men, though, they liked it, especially the young ones.

He received them on the mezzanine of a café that used to be a dance-hall. Downstairs there were racks of records, proper records, vinyl, alongside the counter where the kids ordered their cakes and bacon sarnies. Above, Minos sat enthroned. Leather wing-backed chair. A room, kind of, with a door and three walls, but also more of a landing, with one side nothing but a railing over which you could lean, if you chose, and spit into the teacups of those below.

Minos sat back where he couldn't be seen, but everyone in the building knew when he was there. People coming in one at a time, and going straight up. He smoked, and the café owner let him, however much the others downstairs complained. He'd have his dice-box there ready, next to the cow's-hoof ashtray. The beaker was made of green leather. The dice were big, with rounded edges and corners so that they looked like they'd been carved out of tallow.

'Double or quits?' he'd say.

'You're on,' would say the foot-soldier. A bit of nerves, a bit of bravado.

Minos would let him make the first throw. There was no suggestion that he cheated, ever. Over all, or over a couple of months, say, Minos's gains and losses would balance out, the way the rules of mathematics and of probability decreed that they should. What he was robbing the men of wasn't money. It was the sense that they were entitled to their pay.

Afterwards he'd give the worker a slip of paper, red spot or black on it, and the guy would pass through the frosted glass door by the toilets and down the rusted steps of the fire-escape to the yard where Dee-Dee – his chair and table sheltered by a sheet of corrugated plastic – would check the spot's colour and pay out, or not, accordingly, with his brothers watching from the car.

Dee-Dee's accounting was meticulous. There were of course deductions to be made to cover the cost of next week's merch. Credit was available for those whom the dice hadn't favoured. The terms weren't that easy but he was managing a business here, wasn't he, not a fucking benevolent society. Dee-Dee was a small man, but his brothers (with whom he may or may not have actually shared parents) were not.

*   *   *

The Minoans ruled the west end of the town. That's where the amusement arcades were, and a pink concrete palace set into the side of the cliff, where bands still played summer weekends, and a clock tower with its black-and-silver face.

All along the sweep of the bay, at street level, ran the promenade, its corrugated cement surface speckled with gum-gobs and stained with grease from a summer's worth of chips. Eight broad steps led to the beach, where young women came at the end of their shifts and spread out their towels and crossed their arms to clutch the sides of their dresses, and pulled them over their heads, revealing their almost-bare bodies with a conjuror's flourish. They brought magazines with them, and headphones, and they lay flat on their backs, their bellies concave between the blades of their hip-bones, their voices a muted twittering. One or two of them had babies with them, and they fidgeted ceaselessly, moving the little scraps out of the sun, or straightening their hats, or rubbing lotion into their sausage-link arms.

Men leant on the railing above, looking out to sea apparently but their eyes dropping always, compelled as though by gravity itself. They were lonely and they were lustful. That's normal, isn't it? They didn't talk to each other about it, but they were all engaged in one absorbing game. The game of who-would-you-rather, what-about-blondie-there, how-would-our-babies-look.

Passify didn't sit with the other girls. Minos was king of this town, as he frequently told her, and she was his consort, and the role imposed a certain decorum. Anyway. She didn't particularly want to lie down, there with everybody else, not now she had a bedroom with a gigantic bed in it.

The main beach wasn't her favourite. There were little hopping things that lived in holes in the sand. The rotting seaweed trapped inside the harbour arm smelled rank. It bothered her to see Minos's people – she knew them all – moving through the evening crowd. They looked like everybody else, but they were secretly inauthentic – not really as friendly as they seemed, nor as aimless, nor as carefree.

She could see one leaning on the railing next to one of the Danaans. She knew how it would go. All right? Yeah. Been here long? Not so long, no. Got a job? No, no, no job. You in a doss, are you? Pardon? On the Broadstairs road, like one of those hostels? Yeah. Grim . . . Here's something to cheer you up. And so it went on.

The tide was going out and she could walk all the way she wanted to go on the wet sand, the ridges chilly against her bare soles. She passed beneath the pier, its undersides slimy. Minos had plans for it. He and Dee-Dee talked about it all the time. New amusements, fish-and-chips of course and those cut-outs you stick your head through for photos, and on the end a swank restaurant where honeymoon couples could eat lobster and look at the sea all around, like they were taking a cruise. There'd be a special place, he said, where people could scatter their loved ones' ashes into the water – for a consideration. 'Like walking the plank,' he said. 'You go down the pier, and you don't ever come back.' He was the handsomest man she'd ever kissed, but she didn't kid herself he was kind.

It was dusk by the time she reached the tidal pool. The sea had withdrawn, leaving it a blank rectangle, contained by concrete walls and laid, neat and sharp-edged, among the whorls and encrustations of rock and weed and sand. A man was swimming there alone. From a way off she could see his head, in a red rubber swimming cap, bobbing up and down as he made his way steadily from wall to wall. Swimming lengths. How dreary and dutiful, when the water he swam in had been so lately a part of the churning immensity of the sea. He stood – the water was shallow. He was naked but for his cap and he pulled that off and shook out thick hair almost as red. Paz stood still. He put his clothes on fast and went lightly up the long flight of cliff-steps.

Paz hitched up her skirt and walked in. The lights were coming on. The water around her knees was black and mirror-smooth but, as she disturbed it, it flashed back up at her the lights to which her back was turned. Electric pink electric blue electric green. She waded up and down until the stars came out, singing softly to herself.

Minos said, 'Don't be caught down the East End once it's dark.' She thought he was paranoid, but that was OK, she could go along with it. This time, though, she'd forgotten, or forgotten to care. As she passed the mouth of the gully that led inland, she saw something going on beneath a street-light. Something with an enormous head was lurching there. Going back and forth with arms – forelegs – swinging low. There were two people, standing back and laughing. She thought they wouldn't see her but she remembered how luminous the sea was at night and she froze. The creature stumbled. She saw horns. Its great head seemed to drag it down. Its hind legs were tremulous. It collapsed to the ground and the men stopped their laughing and strolled out of the dark and began to kick it in the belly and the back.

Passify waited for them to be well and truly gone. By the time she waded out through the seaweed at the water's edge her thighs were numb and her toes spongy. She went up the cliff-steps two at a time and took a bus back to the tower where she lived with Minos. Top floor. He liked to be able to look down on the town from above, like a general mounted upon an eminence, surveying the field of victories to come.

Dee-Dee took his breakfast every day in the café between Wonderland and the tower block. It had square plates. He liked the perversity of that. He ate square food. Toast with crusts trimmed off neatly. Sloppy things like scrambled eggs or beans, yes, but always rectified by the toast. The plates were matt black. That was pleasing too.

Paz came in. Minos, at this hour, would be in the gym so she often joined his lieutenant, her face pale and damp-looking from newly applied make-up. She ate square food too. Plastic pots of yoghurt with viscid pureed fruit in triangular reservoirs in their corners.

It was Dee-Dee who had first noticed her. She was as grubby as the rest of the batch when they staggered out of the van, stiff and clumsy as new-born calves. He sent one of the brothers to bring her over to him and she said, 'How much will you give me for it?' Her English wasn't bad at all. He shook his head and said, 'It's not like that this time.'

He drove her back to his villa that night. It interested him how little she seemed to care about being separated from her companions. They'd be down in the tunnels by morning, growing pale under the grow-lights, those that weren't chosen for an induction. He walked her up to the bathroom and he left her there until he realised she had fallen asleep in the bath and he went in through the concealed door, the one at the back of the wardrobe, and for a long time he looked at her, at the blueness of the veins in her breasts and her eyelids, and the fragility of her bones. He got the boys to carry her to the other bedroom and he let her stay there for a night and a day, before he fed her and dressed her and took her to Minos, as a cat brings a dead mouse and lays it on the owner's doormat.

Not that she was dead, far from it. Minos was appreciative.

She said, 'I saw something weird along by the tidal pool last night.'

Dee-Dee had heard about that incident. Somebody had forgotten the demarcation lines, and needed reminding. He said, 'You don't want to be down that way on your own.'

She said, 'The Danaans. There's quite a few of them with red hair, yeah?'

Dee-Dee said, 'Were you swimming?'

'Come on. You know I can't. I was just there. There was a man with like a giant furry turban on his head.'

Dee-Dee arranged his knife and fork, parallel, at a precise forty-five-degree angle to the side of his plate.

Paz had been with Minos nearly eleven weeks. She was used to being told there were things she didn't need to bother herself with. She didn't really expect any answers. She said, 'And something sticking out of it. It was like he had horns.'

Dee-Dee got up and went out the door and made a phone call while she watched him through the plate-glass window, pacing and gesticulating. He came back and sat down opposite her and said, 'Minos and me – we've got to take care of you. We've got plans for you. Did he say? You're going to be running the new club back of town.'

It was what she'd always wanted, a place, glittery and bustling, where she could queen it. When she left the café she saw at once that Dee-Dee's brother was following her – she wasn't a fool. It was worth it, probably. Gain your heart's desire: lose your freedom. That's the story, always has been. She went back up to the flat. Minos frequently came out of the gym wanting what he called a 'warm-down' and he wouldn't be pleased if she wasn't there. Minos's displeasure was often expressed in carnal and distressing ways, and Passify valued her teeth, her straight and dainty nose, her china-smooth complexion.

Later, maybe, after her English lesson, she'd go back to the tidal pool. Surveillance didn't really bother her. Secrets, privacy, they had no particular value. She'd already disappeared more than once. Being known, being noticed, that's what kept you safe.

People washed in and out of the town, and while they were there they were Minos's. They arrived by various means and by diverse routes. It wouldn't do to repeat oneself. One of the boats came ashore on the Ness in the south of the county, and an alarm was raised, and the nuclear power station there bellowed like a gigantic cow in labour while the security guards staggered over the shingle, the beams of their flashlights criss-crossing while the cargo flattened themselves in declivities in the marsh until it was time to crawl to the road where the van was waiting.

They all made it, that lot. Not everybody did. Night-time navigation wasn't easy, what with the currents along that stretch of coast. The agents told them and told them they needed to go empty-handed but they wouldn't sodding listen, would they. If you've got to swim for it, you need your hands free. Even the smallest backpack could drag you down.

The ones who got to Minos's town were put to use, and they were grateful for it. They'd better be. They didn't have a lot of choice. It wasn't cheap bringing them over, as Dee-Dee was frequently obliged to remind them. They had debts to repay. The young women worked in the nail parlours, and they worked (different sort of work) in the parlours' backrooms as well. The men worked down in the tunnels, and weekends they 'spread happiness', as Dee-Dee put it. Week in week out, they were Minos's warriors, fighting with the Danaans for control of the town. When someone crossed a line they'd put the head on him, the manky great bull's head that used to hang in the pub.

The water-meadows inland nourished tremendous cattle. The publican had had the head off his granddad, whose prize bull's it had been. The great brute had once thought with that head and eaten with it and lowered it and swung it and terrified anyone who came near. Now it was hollowed inside. It was heavy. A man could breathe with the head on, but he couldn't lift it off without help and he couldn't eat or drink. Minos found it amusing to watch someone who'd been headed staggering and failing. Passify was right – he wasn't a kind man.

It was Dee-Dee who gave Paz her lessons in English conversation. 'What do you want to talk about?' he'd say, and she'd blather on while he sat drawing her, looking at her very intently but as though she was not actually a human being but an architectural element. His drawings were minutely detailed. He was a finicking man. She was not fooled by his apparent abstraction. She knew he wanted to know everything about her, and she let him have it because no one that she could remember had ever been so interested in her before.

They talked about the club.

'Where I worked in Rotterdam there were mirrors in the floor even,' she said. The journey to this place could be long and tortuous.

'That,' said Dee-Dee, 'is crass. We're aiming for elegance here. We're talking sophisticated.'

'I like a mirrored ceiling, though,' she said, 'that makes you feel high before you've started. And there's all the twinkling and flashing coming at you double.'

Dee-Dee made a note. 'I've never seen you dance,' he said.

'I'd dance for you,' she said.

'Keep talking,' he said. So she told him about how she'd dance with her little brothers, holding them up to her face and kissing their fat cheeks, and how they laughed until they got hiccups. She told him how her mother would call out to her to be careful, not to make them throw up, to stay away from the well. 'Never would she say, "I'm glad they love you. I'm glad you give them a good time." Always "Watch out for this. Careful of that." She didn't like me very much.'

'Is that why you left home?' asked Dee-Dee, holding up his pencil and squinting at her.

Paz scratched at her hair as she did when she was annoyed. 'What do you think,' she said. 'You think I've come all this way just because my mum was cold to me?'

She wondered where her family had ended up after the Minoan agents took her.

Dee-Dee said, 'You've been down the labyrinth?'

She had.

The proposal that the Minoans made was carefully judged. They didn't lie. People in the part of the world where they trawled for fresh flesh weren't going to believe in offers of uncontested immigration and free housing and a decent job. None of that was going to happen, and most of them knew it. They had friends, uncles, people who'd gone before. They weren't fools. They were, on the other hand, desperate. 'We'll get you in,' said Minos's agents. 'But we're not magicians. Work permit, refugee status, benefits – no. Once you're in you can work on that stuff – not our department. But we can use you. Your choice. No obligation. We can use you, and if we do, we take care of you. A place to sleep, some of your own people to work with. And we have an arrangement in place. You won't be bothered by immigration enforcement. Nice to know, don't you think?'

Dee-Dee looked them all over, the young women that got through. They didn't need to look like Helen of Troy, but a certain standard had to be maintained. He got the ones he trusted to take the new recruits in hand. Haircuts, heels, dietary advice. Most of them had been living off some kind of porridge for years, and it showed. He planned the menus in the dormitory. He wouldn't have wanted to eat like that, personally, but he saw to it that it was nutritious. He got them dancing in the backrooms. He observed the way vanity and exercise put a shine on them.

Once they were ready for work they were brought to meet Minos for an induction. The girls very seldom complained, though one or two of the younger ones, each time, needed a slap. That's how Paz had met Minos, being inducted, she and half a dozen others that night. She often thought, what if she hadn't been picked for him. What if she'd ended up with one of the brothers. She wouldn't have been protected like she had been ever since. She'd have gone the way, likely, of the girls who tried to make it to the city, walking up the railway tracks. There'd been an almighty hullaballoo when one of them was found. She'd been headed. The local woman who reported it kept saying, 'I couldn't believe it. I thought I was hallucinating.' It was her dog who'd found the girl, sprawled on the embankment, the heavy hairy head dragging her neck into an unsustainable bend.

'She made a tragic mistake,' said Dee-Dee to the other girls. 'Don't go doing the same, will you. If you're not happy, you need to tell your Uncle Dee-Dee about it. I'm here for you.' The girls didn't say anything. One of them was kid sister to the one who'd gone. Her face was blotched mauve. After the month-end party in the tunnels she walked out to sea, wading nearly a mile through the shallow beige water until at last her feet drifted away from beneath her. The current threw her back on the beach at Ramsgate. 'Silly cow,' said the heftiest of Dee-Dee's brothers.

Back when the town was a fashionable resort, when, at tea-time, in the terraces along the front, professional men and their families would listen to the wireless as they ate jam sandwiches at tables set in the bay windows, and when, at dusk, the brass band would play medleys of patriotic songs, back then, at least once a week, a procession of sacrificial victims would enter the town in the still of dawn. The grazing on the water-meadows inland was lush. Raising beef made sense.

The young cattle all looked pretty much the same. Neat pointed hooves, silky pelts, long pale eyelashes, ears so pinky-clean and soft-looking you'd want to stroke them against your cheek. Before they were weaned they were skittish and playful. Their mothers, no – it's hard work being a cow. Eating enough to sustain your bulk is a full-time occupation. The painfully angled haunches testified to the impossibility of the task they were called upon daily to perform. There was no cladding that knobbly skeleton with fat on a diet of grass alone. But while the dams doggedly ate, their milk-fed young had time to caper, to jump with all four feet together when startled by seagulls, to race in packs, bucking and skittering, from one end of the meadow to the other, male and female together.

Once they were grown, though, their destinies divided. The heifers were let be. They would grow old, or old enough to calve a few times at least, but the bullocks' bodies, rounded and taut with muscle, had been nurtured for another purpose. When the call-up came they went willingly, unsuspecting.

The drovers used lorries mostly, but of a summer's night they'd sometimes still take the steers along the green roads through the marshes, slapping at the midges, chirruping and growling at stragglers as they coaxed the herd towards the yellow glare of the town, while a barn owl, unperturbed by the small noises they made, sailed back and forth across the thistley ground, serenely intent on killing.

It was important to get the animals into the yards at the back of the town, and get the business over with, before people were stirring. No one likes thinking too much about that which has to be done before a fellow can sit down to carve a nice bit of topside for his family, with cabbage and horseradish and Yorkshire pud.

'Slaughterhouse,' said Minos. 'Are you joking me?'

'I'm not proposing you should call the club that,' said Dee-Dee. 'I'm just informing you of the building's previous function.'

Paz was with them. She had made a list, but she didn't expect answers to that many of her questions. Back home she'd helped her mother manage a taverna. Her mother's memory was perfect, because she'd had to rely on it all her life, but Passify could write down the orders and add up the bills. The foreign customers seemed to like that. A list gave one clarity, and a sense of control.

Décor – purple and silver? Wait-staff uniforms same.
Booths – essential
Products for the toilets. Room-fragrance.
Music – DJs – got to pace the night
Lighting *****
Backrooms clean – plenty of tissues
Happy hour

The stars beside the word 'lighting' (she knew that was key) were tiny and neat. When she was first given a pencil she'd spent hours drawing stars on discarded brown paper bags. She could do stars five different ways. Not a particularly useful skill, but she'd acquired it.

She hadn't thought about naming the club. She added that to the list.

Dee-Dee had drawings to show, all done with graphite lines as fine as hairs, on grey-mottled tracing paper. Minos pushed aside the hoof and leant forward to see.

'I want it sophisticated,' he said.

'Have I ever,' said Dee-Dee, 'offered you a proposition that lacked that quality?'

Minos smirked. Dee-Dee was his fixer. The little man's cleverness was his to be proud of, even when it stung him. Paz leaned across to look, so that he could feel the warm dampness of her breath on his hands. After all these weeks, she could turn him on as simple as that. Not often he stuck with one that long.

Dee-Dee talked, and she saw her booths, saw the glass walls that would sparkle with outdoor stars as the lights in the ceiling made stars inside to match them. She saw how the bar curved around the back wall. She saw the stairs leading down to the washrooms. She saw another flight of steps.

'Where's that go?' she asked.

'Tunnel to the labyrinth,' said Minos. 'You don't think I'm walking in off the street?' Minos didn't like the open air. It upset his breathing for one thing. For another, there were often people looking for him, people he wasn't keen to meet.

Cattle-run. Cow-shed. Bull-ring. Beefeater. They liked the idea of calling up the past, and the whiff of meat. In the end, though, they kept it simple. The Cow.

The red-haired man swam every evening in the tidal pool. Paz wasn't there often. It was harder for her to stroll off alone down the beach now she had her bodyguard. But she would see him in the town. He was tall, with narrow hips, broad shoulders and a thick neck. He stepped on the balls of his feet, daintily, like a hoofed thing. The Danaans treated him with deference. Minos's people left him alone. By day he worked in the kebab joint, turning the great lollipops of meat, and slicing fine slivers from them with a knife like a scimitar.

She went in one day. She knew her minder was uneasy but he was never confident of the extent of his authority over her. Surely a girl could be allowed to choose her own lunch.

She said yes to peppers but no to onions, and yes to the tahini and garlic sauce. He didn't look too hard at her. He was exactly courteous. The flatbread was filled, but not overflowing. He wrapped the greaseproof paper around it as though it was a bouquet, fixing it with an ingenious pleat. One of his colleagues was an obstreperous buffoon, always niggling and teasing. She learnt from his banter that the redhead was called Toro. He said very quietly as he handed her the package, 'The tide will be low tonight at eight forty-five.'

It was unusual for her to be unready with something to say, but she just took the doner and nodded, and went off out and down to the waterfront to eat it with her legs dangling against the rough concrete of the harbour wall. Way beneath her the rusty wrecked trawler, on which some of Minos's assets had once tried to escape, broke surface as the tide went out. Minos was out of town.

Dee-Dee's villa was symmetrical. It wasn't that he didn't like a late-Victorian terraced house, such as those that lined the promenade, their superfluity of volutes and pediments and fancy finials making them look, in their dilapidation, like a reef of bleached coral. On the contrary, he was fond of their over-ornamented facades. He liked the whimsical way their balconies' little lead canopies turned up at the corners – some apprentice architect's idea of chinoiserie derived, not from travel, but from looking at willow-pattern teacups. They did very well for others, but for himself he liked a house to be low, and double-fronted, so that when he stood in his hallway the spaces on his left-hand side exactly mirrored those to his right.

He spent his mornings in the study, whose side-window let in the early sun, and his evenings in the sitting room, which was identical in every way except that the chintz curtains were toile de Jouy with milkmaids and cattle, while those in the study were garlanded with bays. There was a kitchen at the back but he seldom used it. When at home, he subsisted

almost entirely on herbal infusions. He liked a steak as much
as the next man, but that didn't mean he wanted to be inhaling
the odour of scorched flesh all night and all day.

Paz chose fennel tea. Nowadays her conversation classes
were pretty much indistinguishable from the conversations she
and Dee-Dee held elsewhere. His drawing of her seemed to be
taking a massively long time, but she didn't have to hold still
for it. He liked to see her on the move. That was cool. She
could do conversation class and work out at the same time.
Any other man, and she'd have thought he just wanted to ogle
her, but Dee-Dee wasn't like that. You couldn't imagine him
naked. You couldn't imagine him touching.

She told him about the redhead. She told him how she
thought of the man at night. Sometimes even when Minos was
with her, on her, in her. For some reason she was sure that
Dee-Dee wouldn't repeat what she told him. He was Minos's
man but there's a limit to what a despot can expect from his
enabler. He and Passify were the favourites, the baskers in the
unreliable warmth of Minos's favour. They had a bond. Besides,
Dee-Dee was an artist. He thought that she was his artefact,
his made thing.

'Where do you meet him?' asked Dee-Dee, applying a char-
coal shadow to his depiction of her hair.

'By the tidal pool, mostly. I'm surprised Bruno hasn't told
you.'

Bruno was the brother who tailed her.

Dee-Dee was cross-hatching, his pencil as sharp as a bee's
sting.

'He probably has told you, I suppose.' She was swinging her
whole torso up and down, arms spread, wide-winged. There

was something liberating about knowing it was impossible to have secrets. It meant indiscretion wasn't reckless, but inevitable.

They weren't assignations, their twilit meetings. Since that first day in the kebab house there'd been no need for either to make a move, to say anything. If she could make it, she was there. He was there always. She'd slip out of her dress and he'd lead her in. He'd swim beneath her while she lightly held his pale shoulders. She discovered what it was to be weightless, to let the water take her.

Dee-Dee said, 'I gather he's quite a dancer. We'll be needing some of those.'

And so it came about that Toro was employed as a greeter in The Cow Club.

Night after night Minos and his favoured associates would come up the steps leading from the labyrinth and sit at the central table. Passify would welcome them, a proper hostess, and slip in beside Minos on the cowhide banquette and put her hand on his thigh. Later she'd leave with him. Later still she'd be back, dancing with Toro, swaying, her wrists crossed behind his powerful neck, her body moving with his as it did in the water. A woman as young as she was doesn't need much sleep. By the time Minos was heaving himself up to go to the gym she was back in the big bed beside him, and the redhead had dived off the pier end and let the current take him eastward, towards the new sun and his tribe's territory.

Paz wasn't such a fool as to imagine Minos didn't know. She thought perhaps he might not care. He wasn't monogamous himself, after all. Lovers are often imprudent, and self-deluding.

It all seemed to be working out fine, until one morning the following spring Minos put his hand on her bump and said, 'Big. I wonder how many babies you've got in there, huh? And how many of them are mine?' His smile was neither affectionate nor reassuring. He said, 'I like my assets to multiply. But you're out of here by tonight.' He kept his voice even. He said 'Scumbag'. He said 'Whore'.

The web of tunnels they called the labyrinth had several entrances. It was so constructed that each section could be separately shut down, transforming it into a sequence of traps. People had been living in those burrows since before there was ever a building above ground. They had kept their cattle in the larger caverns on the landward side. They had watched the sea from the passages that debouched into mid-air, halfway up the cliffs above the beach. They had stored dried meat, and hay, and treasure, in the chilly recesses along the curving walls. There were springs there, where water bubbled up warm and stinking from deep underground, and there was rainwater seeping down from above ground, pooling in basins its flow had carved out from the rock, and running, in grooves it had taken centuries to cut, along the chalky floor.

Whenever an invasion seemed imminent – the Romans, the Norsemen, the Normans, the Spanish, the Dutch, the French, the Germans – farmers would drive their beasts into the tunnels, and anxious men with weapons would explore the labyrinth looking for possibilities of ambush or undermining. Half a century before Passify came to town a gun had been installed in one of the seaward tunnels, its muzzle pointing out at the horizon through an aperture not much bigger than those in which the sand martins made their nests. It had never been fired. People said it was still loaded. The boatmen never much liked to see its glinting eye pressed to the peephole in the chalk cliff.

The incomers who lodged in the labyrinth now weren't marauders. They hadn't come to torch palisades and drive off livestock. They just wanted a place to live. The labyrinth was the holding centre where Minos's crews deposited them, and where they were separated and searched and kept, pending decisions as to their future. Most moved on before the following night. Some troublesome cases took longer. Then there were the tunnels full of synthetic mist and artificial light, where the merchandise was farmed. And of course there was Minos's office, directly under the tower block, where he sat with his scales.

That's where Toro was brought. They yanked at his bound arms, and headed him, and when it was night – obeying Minos's orders – they led him, stumbling under the weight, down the pier to where weeping widows came with their gilded caskets and mass-produced plastic urns. Pay your last respects, they said, jeering. Ashes to ashes. Can you dive, swimmer? They circled around him, prodding and shoving until, in the double darkness inside the bull's head, Toro was lost and amazed and then they shuffled him to the very edge of the planked floor and he fell and, strong as he was, he was dragged down headfirst to the murky bed.

*　　*　　*

The labyrinth was Dee-Dee's pride. Its ventilation, its multiple closable entrances and isolatable chambers, its complicated hydraulics, its electric lighting powered by heat from the earth's core drawn up long slender shafts – all of these were the products of his ingenuity. He had overhauled it and put it into commission for Minos and it befitted the man. Dark, oppressive, intimidating. Personally, Dee-Dee preferred something more rococo.

He had never told Minos about the offshoot of the warren, the grotto that he had found beneath his own villa, and that he had sealed off. A round central chamber with an ivy-wreathed oculus that let in air and dappled light, an encircling gallery. Its walls were encrusted with seashells, not scattered as the sea might have cast them millennia ago, but arranged in complex prissy patterns. There were thousands of shells, perhaps millions. When Dee-Dee first showed it to Passify, months back, she clapped her hands and danced her pleasure in it. Squares and triangles, ovals and spirals, faces with big dark eyes made of mussel shells, bunches of grapes wrought of sea-snails, cornucopias full of flowers each of whose petals was a flawless small powder-pink half-clam.

'Who did it?' she'd asked. 'It must have taken ages and ages.'

'Romans, they think,' said Dee-Dee.

Its secrecy delighted him. He kept a tallboy pushed up against the entrance door. When Passify came to him sobbing he led her down there. There was a bed with oyster satin cushions, there was a basin made of a giant clamshell. There was no risk of anyone hearing her scream, as she might need to. Fortunately he had made a study of obstetrics. He was confident of being able to do the necessary. He always kept his knives sharp. He liked to keep his mind well-honed too, but he did occasionally allow himself a little mental holiday, wafted to dream destinations by an opiate, so his lacquered bathroom cabinet contained the wherewithal to dull the pains of parturition.

By morning there were two babies, a boy with hair the colour of a Hereford bullock, and a sleek dark stocky little girl.

They were found of course. It only took a couple of weeks. Minos came himself, for once, barging into the hallway, sweeping knick-knacks (Georgian brass compass, tortoiseshell ink-stand) off the console table with his beefy elbows. He'd never visited Dee-Dee at home before. The curtains made him laugh. He waved the 'brothers' – his brothers now, not Dee-Dee's – into the little vestibule and while they heaved the furniture about he kept his back turned to his erstwhile right-hand man. Paz came blinking up the steps.

'Got your figure back good and quick,' said Minos. She didn't answer.

A brother brought up the two babies, holding them expertly, one in each crooked arm.

'That's mine,' said Minos, and grabbed hold of the girl, lifting her with his big hands under her armpits. Passify flinched as though it was her own body he had snatched at.

'The other one's yours if you want it,' he said. 'Then you're getting out, the pair of you. You too Dedalus.'

The girl-baby's face was red as she squinted at her father, so loud and overbearing. Her hands waved in the air like tiny star-fish. Passify reached for her.

'No,' he said. 'Mine. Fair's fair. One each.'

Crying did no good. Pleading got her nowhere. She had no leverage, no counter-offer to make. But how could she leave her little girl, whose scalp smelled of cotton and irises, who'd fall asleep clinging to her finger?

Minos didn't want to use force. That would be messy. Paz was, after all, the mother of his child. He offered money, enough to get shot of her. More than enough. But still, there she was, stubborn cow. At last he said, it was almost a joke, but as soon as he'd said it the idea delighted him. 'Right you are then. If that's what you want. Double or quits.'

He was already getting the coin out of his pocket. He handed it to the brother. 'Heads or tails?' he said. Passify shut her eyes. It's the only chance, she thought. Dee-Dee was shaking his head and trying to do something, but what could he possibly do? The gag wrenched his mouth crooked and someone had him in an armlock.

Passify said 'Tails'. The brother tossed. Heads it was.

And so that was it. She wasn't leaving without her babies. Minos didn't much care. He took little Arianna to live with him in the tower and he let Paz come every day to take care of her, so long as she got out of the way when he came in at night with one of the newer girls, or two actually, one to keep the baby quiet while he and the other were in the giant bed, making its leather headboard pound the wall like an angry beast.

Paz would put her copper-headed boy into the buggy, then, and go down in the lift and back to the villa. Dee-Dee had gone Lord knows where. 'Don't worry about me,' he'd said. 'I can fly.' He was a weirdo, but he'd been kind to her. He let her live in the villa 'as caretaker' he said. He wouldn't be back, not likely. She made beds for them in the grotto, the only place the boy felt safe.

When the summer came, she took him down to the tidal pool. Soon he was bold enough to want to swim, and she would launch out into the grey water, the seaweed caressing her belly (not so taut now – no one would ever again want to sketch her as she danced) while he clung to her pale shoulders and butted her with the two little bumps on his forehead. She was glad of what she found in Dee-Dee's well-stocked bathroom cabinet. It helped with the forgetting.

There came a time when she needed more of it. She, who had been queen, joined Minos's sales-team. When the holiday-makers arrived, she'd be there on the promenade, striking up conversations, 'spreading happiness', as though she had a superfluity of the stuff to give away.

JOSEPH

He loved her from the moment she sidled out of the garden door. She was wearing some kind of hairband with glass beads attached, and a swimming costume in two shades of blue – azure above the waist, indigo below. Not that she actually had a waist. At that age the torso is as smoothly unitary as a plum. Her hair was wet. She was barefoot and took little mincing side-to-side steps on the hot paving. She was the most feminine creature he had ever seen, more so even than his grandmother's cat.

She took no notice of him until her father told her to say hello to her Uncle Joseph (he wasn't really her uncle, they were more remotely related) and she held out her hand with no coquetry, as she might have extended it to a door handle – using it to do what needed to be done. Her eyes were at the level of his lowest rib. Her fingers were fat and soft, a little damp, tapering like tiny carrots. He touched them and she said, 'How do you do?' and looked past him towards where her baby brother was on all fours, licking pebbles, and then she looked up at him, fleetingly, and her eyes were pale grey, and from that moment Joseph was hers for life, for ever and ever amen.

He didn't say anything. He went back to London and carried on with the window-cleaning. He lived in a hostel for his compatriots, on the Harrow Road. In the evening, when the others were watching football in the canteen, he walked for miles, learning the city, looking for the perfect place to bring her home to. There was a short street going nowhere, just linking two others, with an apple tree growing from a gap in the pavement. The tree was older, he could tell, than the pavement, older than the gabled brick houses. In April the blossom covered it sumptuously. In September it scattered apples across the tarmac, each with one brilliant scarlet cheek.

In the sixth year after he'd found it he was picking up the apples, as he liked to do, when a man about his age came by. Joseph had seen him before. The man went for a run, every night and every morning, wearing special clothes for running in and carrying a special plastic bottle. He said, 'I've never tried eating them – what are they like?'

Joseph set down his basket and said, 'They are sour.' The man was still watching him, so he went on: 'I like to have them in my room for the colour. And the scent. You understand? All through the winter, day by day, the scent becomes more powerful.'

'So you've been picking them up for years, then,' said the man, who was bending sideways, touching the top of his sock with the tips of his fingers.

'Yes,' said Joseph.

'You must live round here.'

'Yes.'

'In that hostel.'

'Yes.'

The man kept bending from one side to the other, blowing air out of his mouth as though he was being punched in the belly. After a while he said, 'I know this sounds a bit weird, but I don't get much time for getting home-stuff sorted. I'm just wondering. I've seen you around. And I kind of think I could trust you. Do you want to come and live in my house? With me?'

Joseph was a courteous man. He had once been very good-looking. Now his hair was receding it wasn't so much of a problem, but he always found it distressing to be obliged to disappoint. He paused, and chose his words carefully and said, 'It is true that I am not yet married, but I must explain . . .'

'Oh no,' said the man, and actually blushed. 'No. I didn't mean anything like that. You'll meet my girlfriend. I mean. No.'

Joseph smiled and made a placatory gesture, as though smoothing out the unfortunate hump that had jolted their conversation off course.

The man ran his hands over his head and said, 'Look, I'm Geordie. I live over there. The thing is, I need someone to do stuff for me – taking the car to the garage, and all that. Signing for parcels. And I just wondered. I just thought, if you like to make your place nice with the apples . . . Irma's left, you see. You'd have your own room. No rent of course. I go away a lot, but still. And there's the parrot.'

Joseph said, 'I am a window-cleaner. Very skilled and experienced. I am an independent man. My family own orchards.'

Geordie seemed flummoxed. He said, 'Oh orchards. So the apples . . . But you could carry on window-cleaning. It's not a job. It's more like a . . . Well. I mean you wouldn't be a servant.'

The last word hung between them – embarrassing.

Suddenly Geordie shouted, 'Hey!' and began waving. A woman was letting herself into a house across the road. 'That's Lola,' he said. 'My girlfriend.' He said, 'Why don't you come in and take a look?'

Joseph said, 'I will do that. Yes.'

The apple tree had blossomed and fruited twice more before Geordie said one evening, 'I'm being relocated.' He seemed angry. Joseph carried on ironing and waited to find out what this meant for him. 'Nobody even asked if I like Dubai. I hate Dubai. I'm an outdoor person. Lola's going to go ballistic.' Geordie was ricocheting from one side of the laundry room to the other, and there wasn't nearly enough space there to contain his agitation.

'What am I going to do with this house?' he asked. Joseph kept quiet. He wanted to know that, too.

Geordie and Lola broke up. Geordie said the money was too good to say no to. Lola said, 'Even if it means losing me?' and when he didn't immediately answer she began to cry. The truth was they had been very quiet in bed at night for at least a year, which was something of a relief to Joseph – the house's walls were thin. Lola had said to him once, as they made the

shopping list together, 'Didn't you ever want children, Joseph?'
He didn't reply. He considered the question impertinent. He
would never have asked it of her. He knew that she was
thirty-eight.

He was a good window-cleaner. He had never seen the village
from which all four of his grandparents came, but he had
often been told how famous its people were for their immu-
nity from vertigo. The village was in the mountains near to a
frontier that had shifted repeatedly over the last four genera-
tions. Sometimes his people were citizens of this country,
sometimes of that, but always they were the people of that
high village.

He imagined a path with a cliff to one side, a precipice to
another. He imagined a notch in the mountain ridge, the
entrance to a rocky fold filled in winter with snow and covered
in summer with tiny star-shaped flowers. In his mind's eye he
saw pinnacles, carved by the winds of a million years, standing
like sentries way above. He saw, at the head of that hidden
fold, the village clambering up the rock-face. He saw men
stamping on their boots as the sheltering crag caught the first
damson-coloured light, and leading out their goats. He had no
idea where these mind-pictures had come from but he treasured them.

As a matter of course, like all the men of his family who
went abroad, he became a window-cleaner. He contacted his
cousin as soon as he arrived in London and by next morning
he was standing on a windowsill with a plastic bucket and an
implement halfway between a paint-roller and the

windscreen-wiper of a car. Two days later he was left alone in a house. 'I trust you,' said his cousin. 'You're a good boy.'

A sash-cord broke, and he found himself on the outside ledge of the spare room window with no way of getting back inside. The ledge was just wide enough for his two feet placed one behind the other, heel to toe, and it canted very slightly downwards towards the paved terrace three floors down. He leant against the glass and prayed. It was nearly two hours before the woman of the house came out into the garden and saw him there. She called up, but he didn't dare speak, could only whimper. She went back indoors and came upstairs, and yanked the sash up roughly so that he teetered, but she grabbed his shirt and he climbed back into the room. His feet and legs were so cramped he had to slide down the stairs on his backside.

That night he thought, If I had fallen I would never have married her. With window-cleaning there are always risks, but he was careful. All he had to do was stay alive, and make a home.

Geordie went away. Lola took the parrot. She thought it could say her name, although Geordie had told Joseph one night, after Lola had gone to stay with her sister, that what it was actually saying was Rolo. Its previous owner had loved chocolate.

'No point selling,' said Geordie. 'London property's the sweetest place to keep your money. Joe, how'd you like to manage the place if I let it out?'

No one else called Joseph Joe. The name sounded alien to him, but he understood it was intended to be friendly. He wasn't sure what Geordie was proposing. He waited. He was good at eliciting information by remaining silent.

Geordie said, 'All you have to do is let them in, and then check everything before they leave. Clean sheets and a bit of a tidy-up every time there's a change-over. Self-catering – you won't have to cook. You can keep your room. They'll like the service, and you'll let me know if they get out of order. Anything else they ask you to do, they'll have to pay you extra.'

'Extra?' thought Joseph. Geordie had never paid him anything at all. But London rents being what they were . . .

He thought, Now I must ask.

He said, 'I would like the basement, please. I am going to get married.'

The basement had its own entrance. It was dark, as basements are, but a door from its kitchen opened onto a fenced-off part of the garden – a concrete yard with enough space for two chairs. She could plant sage and rosemary in an old ceramic sink out there. It would be a home.

Geordie didn't answer for a while. Instead he pretended to be immensely excited about the forthcoming wedding. He said things like 'You dark horse you' and 'Jesus, that's tremendous'. After a bit he quietened down and said, 'I've never really asked about your private life.' He didn't sound apologetic, only as though he regretted having missed out on something that might have been amusing. He kept jabbering away. Then at last he said, 'Well, I suppose that way we could look for tenants who'd want the whole of the upper house. Lot simpler, and we could still charge short-term rates.' He was ruminating. Talking to himself. 'OK, Joe,' he said, his voice louder, 'the basement's yours for the duration. When's the happy day?'

Duration of what? wondered Joseph, but he thought it was time he trusted to luck. He had savings. He said, 'Thank you, sir.' He knew that it made Geordie uncomfortable to be so addressed but he wanted to signal the formality of their agreement. 'I must go back to my country as soon as possible to make my proposal. Would it be inconvenient if I set off on Saturday?'

Geordie said, 'Wow, you're a fast mover,' but he didn't say no, so the following morning Joseph went to Victoria Bus Station and bought a series of tickets. He could be there and back in a week.

When he told his cousin he would be taking a short holiday the cousin looked irritated. When he explained why, the cousin looked troubled. 'Ioachim's girl?' he said. 'But how have you two been courting? When have you ever met? She is a child, still only a child, in spite of all.' He didn't explain what he meant by the last words.

Joseph said simply, 'I saw her many years ago, and then I made up my mind. She is of age. Now it will be for her to decide.'

'And her parents,' said the cousin.

'And her parents, naturally,' said Joseph.

Every summer her family moved from the high orchards to a small town on the coast. For three months Maria worked in the kitchen of her parents' beachside bar. It was in a clearing in the pinewoods on a rocky shore. Every morning her father rode out from town on his scooter, dragging a trailer loaded with bottled beer and canned fizzy drinks. Maria and her mother went to the market at sunrise, wheeling their bicycles through empty streets where the cobbles were wet from the street cleaner's hosepipe, and loaded their panniers with tomatoes and cucumbers and melons. They pedalled laboriously through the forest, their front wheels skidding on the sandy path, the meat and cheese in their backpacks heavy and damp. As soon as they had unloaded, Maria's mother went back into town – they had another bar there, too, and that needed seeing to – while Maria began to slice and dice and dress the food and her father got the stove fired up. They called it a kitchen, but it was really no more than a patch of sand screened off by a low whitewashed wall.

Her father liked to talk to the tourists. Sometimes the young men leaned over the kitchen's only wall and asked Maria to join them, too. She'd shake her head. 'Thank you, too busy,' she'd say. She made flatbread on the stove, and grilled kebabs on the barbecue. Everyone else there, on the plastic chairs under the pine trees, with the sea only a step or two away, was virtually naked, the men dropping crumbs on hairy thighs, the women wiping fingers, oily from eating olives, on smooth bellies already oily with sun-cream. Maria wore her blue dress, and every night she washed it and spread it out on the flat roof of the cousin's house where they slept. Putting it on damp in the morning made her shiver, but soon it would have shed its moisture and be floating around her legs in a way that made the foreign men watch her movements as attentively as the scrawny cats did. Her hair hung down her back in a long plait.

Septembers, they went back inland to the orchards, for the apricots. Mid-October, Maria returned to school. Her teacher would gather together those she called the 'summer-slaves' – there were several of them in the class – and say, 'Now I have you back again. Now we work.'

Each of them would think, 'Work? She doesn't know the meaning of the word.'

It was the darkest time of year when Joseph came back to see them. Most of the men in the village had found winter employment under the plastic that made the coastal plain shimmer like a lake. Their skin looked sodden. The humidity in the polytunnels made it hard to breathe. But the money wasn't bad. Not bad for winter. And at the end of the week they would bring home sacks of bruised or misshapen tomatoes.

Maria's father took care of himself – he couldn't afford to weaken. As soon as he was home, before he entered the house even, he would go down into the square, the only flat and open space around, and stretch and bend and then run on the spot like a caged creature. The older men smoking on the benches outside the café watched him silently, until one of them said, 'The morning is for effort. The evening is for repose.' Another one spat. A third one said, 'Running away from his trouble at home.' The others looked at this man askance. There are things of which it is not prudent to speak.

*   *   *

Joseph had brought a bottle of whisky, because he knew it was expected, even though Maria's father would not drink it. He had two cashmere jerseys that had not been as expensive as you might suppose (he'd bought them from a market stall). Rose-pink for Maria's mother, the palest pearly grey for Maria herself, because it reminded him of her eyes and of how, once, when she was a tiny child, years younger, even, than she was on the day he had fallen in love, she had said how cosy it would be to be snuggled up in a cloud. And he had the small square box covered in green leather and stamped with gold curlicues, that would not be brought out unless all went well.

He arrived in the village quite early on a Sunday morning. A time when he knew the family would be up and about, but not yet so late that they would feel obliged to invite him to their Sunday dinner, should they not wish to do so. He hoped, of course that they would, that by the time the lamb was roasted he would have a cogent new claim on a place at their table.

The parents were both standing on the patch of ground in front of their low stone house, talking intently. He saw them, as he walked up the hill, long before they saw him, and it was evident they were arguing, not in hostility towards each other, but as allies argue who have a problem before them, and who cannot agree on how it is to be solved. When Joseph was almost within touching distance of them the father turned and laughed harshly and said, 'Then let's hope God will provide,' and as he turned he saw Joseph, and cried out with pleasure, and the two men, who had loved each other since boyhood, began to grasp each other's shoulders, and push each other away, and draw each other forward, and laugh in that way that has nothing to do with amusement, but expresses wonder instead.

Two hours went by. The men sat at the metal table beneath the arbour from whose timbers bunches of red peppers hung. They drank mint tea together, and then beer. The woman kept going back into the kitchen to check on the meat, and coming out again with walnuts, or small dry biscuits, or sliced beetroot.

The men's conversation was repetitive and ceremonious. Both understood, from long experience, how such conversations must go. They exchanged information, but what they were doing was far more than a transfer of data. It was more like a dance, in which participants meet repeatedly, and perform the same movements over and over again, but each time with more energy, until the dancers are loose-limbed and amorous and the atmosphere in the dancing-place – be it room or yard or threshing floor, is so altered that the discrete persons who first entered it merge and become a pool. It takes music, and a night with no pre-ordained ending, for the process to take its full effect, and Joseph knew he did not have so much time, but he felt hopeful. He felt that he had come a good way.

He smiled at Anna, who was Maria's mother, and she smiled kindly too and enquired again about the basement flat he had described, and the little yard with space for herbs. And then she said, because a woman can sometimes presume, and ask the question that must be asked, in a way that's hard for men, 'And who will you live with, there, in your underground home?' And Joseph thought Now! And he said, 'I would like to live there with your daughter Maria.'

And at that moment Maria came in through the gate from the dirt road. She had been to church. Her thick long braid was twined around her head and there were glass beads in it again. A plaid shawl hung across her shoulders but the midday sun was warm and she had let it fall back like wings to either side of her so it was easy to see at once how her belly lifted the front of her faded blue dress.

Joseph stood up. He was pale. He said softly to the parents, 'Please forgive me. Forget what I said. I am too late.' He trembled as he stepped forward to take her hand, saying, 'I am Joseph,' and she said, 'Of course. I know.' And she gave him her hand and her fingers were still short and tapered and he couldn't help it, he stroked them between both his hands, and remembered how once they had reminded him of carrots. And then he bowed, and let himself out of the gate. He had not slept in a bed for nearly three days. He went to the churchyard, not thinking anything, his mind numb, and he lay down under the chestnut tree there and slept until sundown.

When he woke his neck was cricked, but he lay warm under a sheepskin. Anna was near him, her back against a tombstone, darning a sock. When she saw his eyes were open she held out an enamel mug full of tepid milk. It tasted sour and unmistakably animal in origin. From the goat, he thought. He said, 'Thank you.' She said, 'My husband is ashamed. These things are puzzling for men. And this story, this one is strange even for a mother.'

He said, 'I have no claim. There is nothing you have to tell me.'

'There is. There is something.'

'I mean you are not obliged.'

'No.'

She looked up at the sky and the flesh of her face fell back and he saw how beautiful she had been, how beautiful she still must be in her husband's eyes when she lay beneath him.

He said, 'I loved Maria when she was still a child. I have waited until I thought the proper time had come, but I have waited too long.'

'She has no husband. No boyfriend. No one.'

He waited.

'Ioachim and I, we were communists when there was still communism. We do not go to church. She does. Maria. She says that an angel spoke to her. She came to me, very calmly. She told me she had been chosen. That was over a year ago. She was quiet after that, serene, but it was as though she was always elsewhere, waiting for what had been promised. Then, in the summer, something happened on the beach.'

Joseph imagined it. The bar closing up. Maria walking back into town along the rocky bay, wading knee-deep, her blue dress trailing. Phosphorus lighting up as she moved, giving her a spangled train. A man coming up out of the sea, shaking water from his mane. No words. But she, poor deluded girl, ready for him, in proud humility, welcoming.

He said, 'It's monstrous.'

Anna said, 'It will be my grandchild.'

Joseph said, 'I will come back tomorrow. May I speak to her?'

Anna said, 'That will be for her to decide. She is adult, after all. But she will be here. She embroiders blouses and table-mats for the summer-shops. She seldom goes out.' She hesitated, and began to say something. 'She is not . . .'

Joseph interrupted her. 'She is as she is. I loved her when she was a simple child.' He and the mother looked at each other carefully. The word 'simple' vibrated between them.

The conversation that took place the following day was simple too. Both Maria's parents were present, at her request. Joseph proposed marriage. Maria told him candidly, as though she had not imagined the news might have already reached him, that she was pregnant.

He said, 'Because it is your baby, I believe that I can love it. Will you trust me to care for you both?'

She said, 'Yes.'

He said, 'Would you like to tell me who is the baby's father?'

She didn't blush or look down. She was triumphant. She said, 'It is the child of God.'

Joseph sighed and the life he had been preparing with such patience, for over ten years, folded in on itself. He watched it dwindle into a new, sad, small thing. He said, 'I suppose, for those who believe as you do, we are all God's children.'

She looked up and those strange pale eyes of hers were wide as she turned them on him, and she said, 'Yes.'

By the time the blossom was on the apple tree again, Geordie had returned. He said, 'I know it's not the best time to do this to you, but Yolanda works from home, you see, so the base-ment . . .' Yolanda was his new partner – people didn't use the word girlfriend any more. She advised other women what make-up to put on their faces. Until they moved out, Joseph and Maria had to answer the door repeatedly to couriers delivering packages full of complimentary lipsticks for her, and to show her clients into the dining area, which had to be cleared of all food and drink by 9 a.m. A consulting room in the basement, with separate entrance, would be much more convenient.

Joseph and Maria walked together to the hostel where he used to live, but the manager looked at her belly and said, 'Sorry, mate. No kids.' It was only on the very day before Geordie wanted them out that Joseph found work on a farm in Kent. The picking season wouldn't start for another month but the employer said, 'I'm a mother myself. You can come and live in the van right away. There's no heat, mind. And I hope your wife won't be bothered by the cows.' Once the baby was born Maria learnt to pod peas with one hand while breast-feeding. Summer was OK. But one night Joseph said to her, as gently as he could, 'Maria. I don't know. I don't know how we'll live once the apple-picking's done.'

She and the baby looked at him with their matching pale grey eyes, and she said, 'I trust you.'

He went back to the window-cleaning, even though his cousin wasn't getting so much work now. He was afraid, as he had never been since that day he had shut himself out. Once he dropped his bucket from a bedroom sill, and broke a glass panel in the conservatory roof, and had to pay for it. His hands were often slippery with sweat. On the ladder, his knees trembled. When he came home to the room he'd rented he'd see those two looking at him as though from further and further away. They were so alike there was no telling what kind of a man the father might have been. Joseph felt alone, as he never had in all the years of anticipatory love.

Once, walking down the short street on his way back from work (it wasn't really on his way, but he liked to take that route) and seeing the apple tree in blossom again, he sat down on the low wall around Geordie's front garden, and thought about God, and goodness, and how he had always tried to do the good thing, and how he had always expected good to come of it, and how he no longer thought that it would, or not for him anyway, and he stayed there for a long time, muttering words he would never normally use.

At last he broke off three flowery sprays to carry back to her, hoping to please her and the child, but the petals fell off one by one so that by the time he reached their door there were none left, none at all, on the gnarled black twigs.

MARY MAGDALEN

No touching, he said. No problem, I said. So we mimed dancing. Leaning parallel, slantwise, as in an italic legs-eleven. Our heads dipped sideways in unison. Our palms came as close as close can be without clapping, but never clapped. Our midriffs moved alongside each other, buffered by an inch of empty air. We never kicked, never brushed ankles, never stumbled or said Excuse me. He rested his chin, not on my head but on my halo. My hand floated, light as a scrap of blown paper, not on his shoulder but on his shoulder's aura of exuded body-heat. There would be no noisy slapping of perspiring flesh between us, no struggle or grunt.

That was all right with me. All day I touch. I get plenty of it. My fingers prod flesh, and manipulate it, and cosset it, and hurt it. I yank out hair from chins and nostrils and armpits. It smarts, I know it does, I've had it done myself. I know that as I rip the wax away, bringing the bristles up by their roots, I rip tears from the tear ducts, to flood the clients' eyes. They strip so I can tweezer around their nipples. The itsy-bitsy garments the girls wear used to be called *cache-sexes*, but they're not much use for hiding anything. Women sprawl, legs splayed, while I rid them of their pubic hair.

Shameless. That's one of the pleasures of it for them. It's warm in the salon. There are no windows in the treatment rooms, no possibility of peeping. I move towels around – ostentatiously clean ones, folded neat as new. These towels, draped over whichever part I'm not working on, are supposed to spare us all embarrassment – but where's the modesty in discreetly covering your top while I'm extracting follicles from your arse-crack? I am far more intimately acquainted with the bodies of those I treat at Willesden Beauty, than I am with those I service up the cemetery.

I met him in the pub. I like the corner table. I like the men who stand in groups and make noise, not for purposes of communication but to show affection for each other. Got you! They holler. Nice one! Hear that, Andy? Sometimes they glance my way, but I've got my light dimmed. Just someone in the corner with a kindle. I'm not that much of a reader. But I do like to get inside someone else's head in my off-time.

I am completely undefended when I am around him. I am wholly attent. So when we walked into The Lamb I knew at once that he had taken in the woman reading alone. Taken in, as in noticed. Taken in, as in offered a refuge and a home in his heart. Taken in, as in fooled like he'd fooled me. There's really not much joy in being loved by someone who loves pretty well every loser who crosses his path.

We did what we do. He stands near the middle of the room, doing nothing much until everyone in the place is staring at him.

I buy the drinks. Peter and the others spread out, smiling, being a bit flirty with the women nattering in pairs, saying All right? to the huddles of men.

She carried on reading. She was about his age, I'd guess. Not a kid. When I handed him his ginger ale he said OK, John? and took the vodka-tonic as well, the one I'd meant for myself, and pulled out the chair beside her and offered her the drink. She looked up like she'd been asleep and went to shake her head and shoo him away, then didn't. He stayed, sitting in that very upright way he does, as though his spine is a radio antenna and he's picking up a signal.

They talked a bit. There's a jukebox in that pub. It's always the men choosing. Does every man want to be a DJ? And it's the girls who go out on the floor first, in threes and fours, and begin to shimmy. I was dancing with Ben, doing little twitchy robot moves, mirroring each other, when I saw him stand, and gesture 'after you' to her, and saw her stow her rucksack under the seat and then step out and turn to him and begin to lead him in a dance so rightly calibrated it was as though the two of them were twins, or entwined serpents. Or lovers, I thought, but that wasn't going to happen, was it?

We danced for nearly two hours that night. He was fit, sure. I could see the other women in the place eyeing him, but we were putting on such an act they could see there was no prising him away.

I swim, mostly, for exercise. I go to the pool when I'm done in the cemetery, and take a shower so hot it's like I'm scalding the night off me. I'm usually alone there until six-ish when the suits come in for their pre-work workout. Idea was, it would be good for thinking. Me-time. Meditation. But all that goes through my mind are numbers. Counting the strokes on my back so I don't break my skull on the pool-wall. Counting the strokes forward for no earthly reason but that my mind's in neutral, and seventeen eighteen nineteen are about the most emotionally neutral words I know. I danced like that, without thinking about it, and it turns out that when mind stops interfering body knows what to do. Sex was like that once, between getting it all wrong, and learning how to do it to a professional standard. There was an in-between time, a good, brainless time. That was before I started working.

When they began calling Time I said Thank you, just that. I don't recall him saying anything. I went into the ladies and took off the T-shirt and washed myself down. Make-up. Lots. The light's low where I'll be. Subtlety is not the way to go. Leather jacket back on over nothing much. Undo the plait and let the hair hang down. It's long. Loose hair. Loose behaviour. The connection's as old as hypocrisy. First thing they do to the nuns is shave it all off. High heels in the bag – I'd got a walk to do.

By the time I came out the jukebox's flashing lights were off. He was gone. He and all his friends. I'd seen that dark one's jealous eyes on me all night. I went up the Lane, going slow because my feet were sore, and I took the spot between the snazzy new bar and the gap in the cemetery wall. Prime location. The other girls know that if they see me coming they have to vacate it pretty damn quick.

*   *   *

John, he said. That was ominous. He didn't use names much. I sometimes wondered whether he even knew us one from t'other. I'm afraid I've disappointed you, he said to me. Nope. You can't be disappointed without having been hopeful – and I wasn't. Not ever. He didn't want anything from me, and he wouldn't take anything either. He was sufficient unto himself. I dreamt about him – voracious, lusty dreams – but the thought that I might one day be allowed to touch his hidden skin, it never crossed my waking mind for one moment. Nor the idea that he'd singled me out, though others thought so. So, no, not disappointed as such.

We were in the cemetery. It was one of our places. It was a good place to meet. In daylight people walked their dogs there. After dark different people came in through the broken bit of the wall and got up to all sorts. There were benches, wrought iron, uncomfortable. Sometimes you'd see a mourner, her swollen feet pinched by best shoes, sitting still for hours. There was a small man, quite old, dapper, in a spotted cravat, who came every day with his terrier and fussed around putting flowers on a grave. His dog lapped water from the basin on the tomb next door, into which a fibreglass cherub poured water from a conch. There were inscriptions made of tissue paper and tinsel, blocky great capital letters like shouts – DAD, GRAN, OUR MUM – as though the bereaved were yelling at their oldsters to come on down and eat their tea. People looked at us sideways and kept their distance. Most people find a group of young men hanging out scary. I can't pretend we were all that clean.

He was done in. He sat down on a bench and folded his hands and rocked his head back. Eyes closed. I thought he was shutting us out, seizing a bit of alone-time. You couldn't blame him. It was getting pretty intense. Lucky thing the woman was there.

I was getting sloppy. Fair enough, I was tired. Anyone would be. But time was I made a point of getting back to my place – whatever place I had, there've been a few. I'd stopped the swimming when they put the membership up. Actually no. Tell the truth. I stopped when a man standing next to me in the trough full of chlorine said – soft, so no one else could hear – I remember that tattoo, don't I? Magdalen? (I have a number of names.) So I never went again.

Change shoes, jog back to the boarding house, clothes off, make-up off, the shower, using the hand-held to sluice out my fanny, teeth, pills, plait hair, bed, and then a good two hours, with luck, before I started to hear other lodgers grumbling to each other as they queued for the bathroom. All they liked to talk about was the racket from the bar downstairs, and how it had kept them up all night. Self-righteous whingers. Inconsiderate, that's the word they used over and over. They never stopped to consider that I might be there, my head only inches away beyond a partition made of plastic-coated air, that I might be near to hallucinating with exhaustion.

Anyway that spring I left off the routine piece by piece. Teeth – forgot them. Make-up – it's not as though I was laying my head down on a freshly ironed linen pillowcase anyhow. Plait – what made me think I was a goat girl in a dirndl? And then, eventually, bed – who needs it? It was getting warmer. I'd save on the rent. There was a shed for when it rained. I had my down-coat, didn't I? The stone slabs were hard but flat. I lay on them with my hands folded in front, like a customer ready for a wax.

There was a woman who came most mornings. She had four dogs. Two tiny ones with spiteful pointed faces. She dressed them in coats made from her own discarded pink quilted dressing gowns. Two bigger. All rescue dogs. Neurotic. The halt and the lame. She sat dozing in the sun and the dogs sat around and stared at her. There were hard biscuits in her pocket, smelling of Marmite. The dogs kept their eyes on her as though, by willpower or by mesmeric force, they could set those nuggets flying into their own mouths. I watched them and laughed and then stopped laughing. The way we all sat round and stared at him – not much different.

I didn't know Magda when she came by. She was wearing one of those coats that looks like a sleeping bag. I think she used it that way. The hood was up with snakes of her hair wriggling out around her jaw. She tripped over me as she went to grab him. She said Christ don't you care about him? I thought you were his posse. His head lolled back and flopped one way and another. She said You and you, get a hold of his shoulders. Support his head for Christ's sake. Keep it steady. Now lean him forward. Slow. Head down. That's it.

His face was white and matt as a peeled mushroom. She knelt between his knees and breathed into his face. She never touched him. It can't have been coyness, not given what she'd been up to in that place. Just yelled at us to move him around like the bendy-man I had when I was a kid going from one foster home to another.

Going to sit there staring at him all day, were you? She was hissing. His head dangled. There was a sad bony knob at the base of his neck and two tendons as delicate as wings straining against the downward drag of gravity. She pushed back her hood and her hair fell down either side of him, cloaking his face and resting on his sprawled-open legs. Amazing hair, yellow and crinkled, it reached the hem of the little leather skirt she wore at night. She slumped back onto her heels and ducked forward so she could hear his breathing. She must have knelt like that between men's knees often enough. That hair was coiling around his calves now, lapping at his trainers. She made us take the shoes off and got Stephen, who's good at that kind of thing, to massage his calves and ankles and then his feet. They were as dainty as a unicorn's hoofs, and as lifeless. And all the time Stephen worked she was sitting so close that her hair was tangling around his hands. Sorry, he said, over and over. Sorry what? she said. I'm pulling your hair, Steve said. It was wrapped around his feet now. She said, It's not hurting. It's the closest I'm ever going to get to him. I'll give him some stuff.

She pulled herself up and sat on the bench beside his slumped body, their thighs three inches apart, and brought out a wrap, a mirror, a razor blade. When she handed me the glass, a silvery round the size of a digestive biscuit, there was the neatest of lines laid across it. I licked my finger and dabbed it on his gums and after a few seconds he stirred and moaned and muttered.

We were rattled. We'd had to imagine for a minute or two how we'd be without him. What would be the point of us? Mark and Luke, they had big ideas, but the rest of us, we just tagged along with him. When he sat up we went to thank her, and one or two of the guys wanted to ask had she any more of that gear? But she was gone. She was angry. Some of our lot had been making

ignorant remarks about her. It's not as though they were exactly
celibate themselves.

The next time I saw him he was being dragged through the cemetery. Big louts, one each to each of his limbs. They lifted him so that his shoulders must have been dislocated. They dropped his legs and ran with him so that those feet, that I'd seen bare only that once before, bounced over the ground. He was passive. That was his way. He was impressive but he didn't want to impress, to leave an impression on people. He wanted to pull out what was in them. And what was in these lads was anger.

Or perhaps he was just helpless. Certainly I wasn't helping. I wouldn't have dared. They all got his legs next and swung his upper body so that his head bashed against slabs of black shiny marble. I stayed in the far corner with the old women twittering there. A couple of terriers were running with the group, yapping. One man kicked out at them so that he lost his balance and fell awkwardly, dragging the leg he was carrying into an angle it was never meant to reach.

I was shaking so hard I had to crouch down. I got under the crooked yew tree, where the ground's always dry, and lay there. My hands were numb. I was convulsing, my whole body flapping where it lay like a desperate fish. When it stopped I fell asleep, there where I was, and my mind plummeted down into the dark.

*   *   *

Peter was the bravest. He stayed around. All that day till midnight he was going from pub to bar to barbershop. He wanted to know why it happened. He nearly got taken himself. But what was the point of that? It was too late to make any kind of deal. The rest of us split. It was left up to Double-M, as we called her. She was the only one of us to be still there the morning after. She saw a couple of them come back at first light and start digging a hole. It was dismal weather. The hole kept filling with water, and its sides collapsed. Three times that happened, before they gave up. They heaved aside a slab from one of those mausoleums that look like little houses. They lifted his broken body inside and dumped it on a kind of ledge thing. Then they got back in their transit and drove off, windows up, radio on.

I went out through the gap in the wall as soon as the van was gone. It was Saturday, and once the cemetery was properly open it would fill up with little kids on scooters punting along behind the dads jogging. I walked around all day and then I bought some wine and pitta bread. I had a confused idea that I ought to celebrate. He'd never screamed, never whimpered. I call that something. So that night I crept back. There were girls doing business but we never take any notice of each other, even if we're opposite sides of the same tree. I slept up against the wall of his little house.

Sunday morning I drank from the standpipe they used to water the primulas on the graves. I tied my hair back and picked the sleeping dust out of my eyes. I peed round behind the clump of hazels. I composed myself. Tending bodies was my speciality. This was something I could usefully do. I went to the house of the dead and peered into the darkness. I could see his jacket – blue and yellow. It lay there, bundled up as though to cushion his poor smashed skull, but he was gone. That long, thin body had gone.

I crawled into the darkness and howled. What does it matter? said mind. He's dead anyway. You know that. You're not getting him back. Your relations were not physical, ever. You never so much as ran a finger over his collarbone or fluttered your eyelash against his cheek. What does it matter where his carcass has gone? That was mind's view. But body remembered how we had danced. Body said his shoulders were broad and his fingers were pale and there was a way the flesh around his jaw furrowed when he smiled that got me every time. I sat and thought about it until my feet were numb and then I stepped out and I saw someone else.

When I was about three, or young enough anyway to need my mum to be in my field of vision the whole time, like every second of every minute of the day, I was in the park with her, and I was watching some ants coming up out of a hole in the earth. They found a biscuit-crumb, and they got together in a great disciplined work-gang and tugged it – it was like a boulder as big as a house door for them – back to the hole, and the hole wasn't big enough. They tried one way and they tried another way, and it was about the most fascinating thing I had ever seen, these tiny creatures so hard at work.

I couldn't stop myself. I put out my finger and touched the crumb. I was horrified because I had gone in my mind into the ants' world but my poking finger was like a giant's and at once I was back to being human-sized again and I looked up and there was my mother walking away and I ran as fast as I could after her, but that wasn't very fast because my sandals were undone and I couldn't keep up and I began to cry so loud the person looked round and she was just like my mother but I didn't know her, or I knew her but I knew I was wrong to, because it wasn't really her. It was a woman her sort of age and wearing her sort of jeans. You don't really know what your mother looks like when you're that young. She's too much a part of you for you to step back and see her face. This woman was kind. She knelt down and said, Breathe very slowly. Pretend you're an elephant and the air has to come all the way up your long trunk. If you do that you'll be able to stop crying and then we can look for your mummy. But I was too distraught to pretend anything.

My mother found us, and knelt down with the not-her woman and said Meg. Meg. Megalump. Quietly now. And my howling shuddered and slowed but I was still afraid because I looked at the two women and I saw long brown hair and faces pink from the sun and similar T-shirts and I thought, How do you tell the difference? How can I be certain sure which one is mine?

I did lose my mother later, but that's not what I'm talking about. I don't believe in presentiments.

So, there was a man. He worked in the cemetery. Would you call him a gardener or a caretaker or a keeper? Whatever, those are all good words for him. He didn't seem to think it was up to him to make judgments. He dragged away the fallen branches and threw out the dead flowers and cleared the brambles and binned the condoms and beer cans and sometimes I'd see him in his tool-shed, sitting rather hunched on the seat of a ride-on mower, and with his big fingers he was stitching away at a bit of coarse brown canvas, wools in old-rose and olive-green and silvery-blue trailing from his hands. I didn't know his name, nor he mine, but that was all right. That wasn't necessary.

There were others who worked there, who shouted at each other, and made their machines roar. This one was matey enough with them but no more than that. He'd be there suddenly. You never heard him coming. And that morning, he was there. That's what I thought. I said, Did you hear what happened? Any of the others, I'd have been afraid to make them think I was involved. But I didn't mind him.

He didn't answer. He looked at me, that's all. Very still. Passive. And then I knew it wasn't him. It was him.

The world went silent. My mind slipped out of gear as it does as you're going to sleep. I believed everything and nothing. I thought this changes everything. I thought this is a blind alley in time with no significance and no consequences. I thought this is what joy feels like, so. I thought about my mother, and that other woman and the no-difference between them. I held out a hand. He took a dancing step towards me, one foot crossing over in front of the other in an unstable beautiful move from which you could only fall or fly away.

He said, No touching. No problem, I said.

TRISTAN

'You'll have to go and meet her.'
  'Why? Is she a half-wit?'
'Her flight gets in at eleven fifty-five. Find her. Be sweet. Take her to lunch in Windsor – she'll like that.'
'What makes you think she'll like it?'
'Then bring her back here. Why are you being like this? It's a question of politeness.'
'Why can't she just get the train. Is she a cripple or something?'
'She's physically perfect. As near to perfect as it's possible to be.'
'What's she coming for?'
'To marry me.'
'What the fuck? Are you joking?'
'No. This is real.'
Silence
'Why aren't you meeting her then?'
'You know I can't. Not with the Fair on.'
'You won't miss half a day's business for her, and you expect her to marry you.'

'It's a pity but . . . We discussed it. She knows I have to work. She kind of likes it. She likes knowing her man is this big busy deal-maker.'

'She doesn't. Nobody would. You've got to be there when she comes through the gate. Next to all the drivers with their bits of cardboard. You put your hand on the barrier and you vault lightly over it and you put your arms around her and lift her up so her feet are two inches off the floor and you bury your face in the side of her neck and she's dropping things – passport, wallet, everything, the duty-free vodka, and you say . . .'

'She's actually appreciably taller than me.'

'Oh. Oh. In that case I have to revise all my ideas. In that case you stand quite still at the end of the barrier and let her come to you, and she walks with long easy strides, she lopes, and she's wearing a linen dress that's like a coat and it billows out behind her and it's unbuttoned at the front so that her legs are half bare and they're burnished like bronze swords and she doesn't wear jewellery but there's a leather thong around her neck and when she reaches you she puts a hand on your shoulder and she dips her head and she bites . . .'

'Shut up, Tristan. She is actually a real person.'

'Yes? So? Where did I say she wasn't?'

'She's real so there's no need to make her up.'

'I like making people up. The people I make up are much more amusing.'

'More amusing than . . .?'

'More amusing than you, you literal-minded old faggot.'

'No more cheek. And no more homophobic language. I'm getting married.'

'So you say.'

'That's right.'

Silence

'And have you considered the possibility – has it crossed your mind for even one single second – and if it did would you give a toss about it – has it occurred to you that if you really are doing this thing, then you might be breaking my heart?'

'Eleven fifty-five. Terminal 3. Car keys on the hall table. Have dinner with us tonight.'

'Us?'

'With me and my girl.'

The things that Mark Cornwall bought and sold were – at least purportedly – very old indeed. Their monetary value was more closely related to their antiquity than to their beauty. His regular clients liked to hold an Egyptian basalt hawk, or an agate bull from Mesopotamia, and feel the centuries thrumming through the stone. No matter that the carving tended to be crude and the creatures depicted barely identifiable in the lumpen forms. You didn't have to be superstitious to feel the potency of a thing that had been held and treasured and very, very gradually worn away by the stroking hands of generation upon generation of long-dead human beings.

To get the non-specialist buyers in, though, you needed some straightforwardly lovely stuff. Alabaster always looked good, so long as you knew how to light it (Mark's tech-guy really, really did). Fragments of Roman wall-paintings for colour. A Macedonian gold tiara for flash. Anything that had once been animate got attention. Mark had recently been amassing a stock of mammoths' bones. Dutch trawlers brought them up in their nets from the bed of the North Sea. Quite a few people were interested. The big draw at his stall at this year's Fair, more popular even than the tiny silken shoe of a Han dynasty princess, was the shoulder blade of a bison scratched all over with twig-like bipeds – a three-thousand-year-old hunting scene depicted by the predator on a left-over part of the prey.

Mark was nervous, which was a condition so unfamiliar to him that he initially mistook it for oxygen-deprivation. 'I'm going out for a breather,' he said to the intern. 'Text me at once if anyone looks like they're getting serious.' The intern had a vapid face, but there was something about the turn of her neck that reminded him of Izza and he felt the ground shift beneath him again. 'Back in ten,' he said.

The park was full of football games. He stood on the temporary decking outside the Art Fair's enormous marquee and watched groups of boys running, red-faced and determined, around and about each other. Viewed from above, he thought, they would have made swirling centripetal shapes, kinetic art. From his viewpoint they merely looked desperate.

Kurt was there – fellow-dealer, rival, nosey-parker. He started to say something. Mark knew in advance the tenor of it – some innuendo about the footballers – and wanted nothing to do with it.

'Congratulate me,' he said. 'I'm getting married.'

'You?' said Kurt, as though the first person singular pronoun might possibly have applied to someone else. 'I had no idea you and Tristan had got that far.'

'She's called Izza,' said Mark. 'I saw her at the Biennale. She's arriving today.'

'Christ,' said Kurt. 'You're not serious? You are serious. But you're not . . .'

'The marrying kind? Turns out I am. Tristan's at Heathrow now, picking her up.'

'You sent Tristan?'

'Sure. They're the same age. Nice for her.'

'But not so nice for Tristan. The boy must be devastated.'

'Oh well. He'll live.'

Kurt looked at him for a couple of beats. 'You are a reptile, Mark Cornwall.'

Mark said, 'Hang on. I'm just a station he stopped off at.'

Kurt said, 'On the whole I'd say an absence of vanity was a positive attribute, but this is callous. You don't know the effect you have on people.'

'My oh my. Are you owning up to being besotted with me, Kurt?'

'You shit.'

The two men each put an arm across the other's shoulder, and they walked together back into the Fair.

Naturally enough, Tristan was expecting an androgynous being with a shaved head poised on a long etiolated body. Something not unlike the Ife terracotta deity (awfully late for Mark, but aesthetically bang up his street) that stood on the first-floor landing in the Little Boltons. Tristan wasn't ready for the woman walking towards him, looking as though she was about to cry, or perhaps was already crying. He hadn't imagined her to be someone he would ever get to know, so he had been staring at her shamelessly and without any kind of greeting on his face or welcome in his posture. She was pretty much right on top of him when she began speaking. On top, yes, because Mark was right, she really was tall.

'Do you get met at airports often? I never have. I'd never thought. It's so difficult isn't it, getting the right expression on your face as you come through those doors? Did you think it was me? Of course not. Obviously. How could you know? And how to handle the luggage. It's so awkward. This is Bronwen. Mark said you live with him. He implied he had teams of ephebes and so forth to fetch and carry for him, but I'm not going to be surprised if they turn out to be figments. Are you one of legions?'

Which, if any, of her questions required an answer? Tristan said, 'I'm Tristan.'

Izza said, 'Isolde.'

Bronwen, neatly packaged in denim, was as compact as Isolde was wafty. She said, 'You take this one, would you?' and passed him the handle of one of the two immense mauve metal suitcases she'd been trundling. 'You brought a car?' He hadn't expected another person. There was a lot about this encounter for which he hadn't been prepared.

Isolde, if that was what she was really called, looked like a bride. Not that she was in a big white dress, although her clothes were much more in evidence, more in need of tossing and twitching and generally tending, than the sleek suits and close-fitting dresses of the women who hung around the gallery. It was more the impression she gave of being entirely, defencelessly, on offer that was bridal. Her face was pale and the skin on it looked damp, as though she had been newly peeled. Her lips trembled slightly as she talked. Her large pale eyes shifted and misted, suggesting she needed glasses, not to see with, but to provide protective cover. Tristan thought that she would never initiate a contact, a relationship, a love affair, but always wait to be found, and that sometimes the person who sought her out might not wish her well, and that she was aware of that danger. Ungainly, superior, nervous, she reminded him of a horse he sometimes groomed. He had many little jobs.

She said, 'Where's Mark?'

'Didn't he tell you, the Fair?'

Evidently Mark had not told her.

Bronwen stood silently waiting for something to resolve itself.

Tristan said, 'Mark thought you might like to go to Windsor, have lunch. He'll be through by evening.' He was beginning to rather like the idea of an afternoon in the Great Park with these odd young women. 'I brought a picnic.'

Again that look of imminent tears. He'd get used to it. It didn't signal grief. Bronwen took over. 'Let's do it then. I can't stand these places. You're in short-stay?'

She set off in the right direction. He followed and so did Izza, talking in her breathy, curiously elderly voice, telling some story that, what with the recorded announcements, and the rattle of the suitcases' wheels, he couldn't follow. Something about someone getting injured in Venice, and her nursing him, and Mark being tied up in it somehow. How trite, he thought. Didn't Mark know that everyone falls in love with nurses? It's fear that triggers it, and then euphoria at being still alive, and so you think some perfectly ordinary overworked health-worker is your delivering angel. And when you go back for your check-up you get a bit of a jolt to see how they no longer have a halo, just grey panda-rings around their exhausted eyes. His interest in exploring ways of altering his consciousness had occasioned quite a few trips to A&E. After his last little mishap he'd actually made a date with an anaesthetist. Mistake.

The Great Park, where kings have been hunting down stags and damsels for two millennia, is surrounded by mile upon mile of suburbia, of pebble-dash semis and harsh, unweathered red-brick mansions with high walls and electronic gates and security cameras that crane their necks to follow visitors up the driveways like dispassionate predatory birds. Even inside the park there are clumps of housing scattered among the clumps of trees. But for all the way that modern Outer London has infiltrated it, the park is still a wilderness. It is not hard at all to get lost there.

'I think if we go that way we'll get to the Long Walk,' said Tristan, who was prone to claustrophobia. He wanted openness and majestic scale, not fidgety changes of mood between pinewoods and pools of bracken and driveways leading to Tudorbethan houses in bosky glades. Bronwen went ahead the way he indicated, hands clutching rucksack straps. Her gait was as neat and purposeful as the rest of her demeanour. Would she, he wondered, be moving into the Little Boltons as well? He rather hoped so. Izza's softness and scattiness was beginning to tire him. Her conversation was elaborate. She was clever, obviously. She made sure everyone knew that. But she was also, he thought, helpless as a baby, and needed almost as much attention. Bronwen, like a confident nanny, was quite brusque with her. It was obvious they adored each other. Did Mark know that Bronwen looked like being a part of the marital ménage? Did Mark know anything?

'So, when did you meet Mark?'

'Oh, we haven't actually met.'

'But aren't you . . .?'

'Getting married? Yes, it's too impossibly silly, isn't it.'

They were picking their way now between lightning-struck oaks, their charred and riven trunks festooned with irrepressible green. 'He wrote to me about the accident, you see, and I wrote back, and long after there was anything for us to discuss these emails kept pinging back and forth. Very long ones from me because, as you may possibly have noticed, I am a babbling brook in human form, and laconic, witty short ones from Mark, and then just as I was thinking I really should stop wasting this man's time with my reflections on this that and the other thing, he suddenly wrote, "I think we should get married, don't you?" And he probably just meant it as a rhetorical flourish, but I thought Yes, Yes, and then we could carry on this conversation night and day and well . . . "the marriage of true minds". So, met, no, we haven't yet. It's actually kind of clarifying not to have any idea how he smells or to be aware of any of that mind-fuddling carnal stuff.'

Bronwen had found a perfectly circular dell and was sitting cross-legged at the centre of it. They paced around her, Tristan too agitated to settle.

'But marriage. I mean. Suppose you don't find him attractive.'

'Oh, sex. Well. It's not very difficult, is it? I mean guinea pigs do it all the time. Actually, guinea pigs are very clever, they can virtually talk. But llamas too. And God knows what. I've always been rather in favour of arranged marriage, haven't you, it cuts out all that shy-making courtship. And failing a Pandar to arrange one for me, I thought let's give it a go. I mean people manage to procreate, don't they, without having felt they were drowning in the deep deep pools of a lover's eyes or whatever. Haven't you ever had sex with someone you hadn't previously found physically attractive?'

Oh yes. Yes, he had. Tristan had done that often enough. He didn't reply. He laughed it off. This woman might be verbally incontinent, but he knew how to keep his thoughts to himself. He spread his jacket gallantly, and when she folded herself down, ignoring it, he sat himself neatly on its denim square.

Tristan had brought sausage rolls and salmon quiche and cold asparagus and punnets of tiny tomatoes, yellow and red, and a bottle of rather good white and one of mineral water, and proper glasses to drink them out of (but only two because he hadn't been aware of the existence of Bronwen – the women shared). For afters there was bitter chocolate and a bag of cherries. This is what Mark liked to have on a picnic, and Tristan had seen no need to vary the formula. Bronwen had brought three pale pink tablets. Fourteen minutes after they had taken them Tristan and Izza were deeply, ecstatically, helplessly in love.

Love swept Izza up onto her feet and blew her, a tossed veil, spinning around the dell. She wasn't small but her movements were airy. She undulated. She drifted. Tristan danced after her. As Mark had sometimes observed (not always kindly) he was a natural-born partner, a lifter and catcher, a twirler and supporter of more sparkling beings. As the prince or woodcutter's son kneels, his legs well-muscled in tights, so that the ballerina can use his thigh as a mounting block to spring up from, Tristan was obliging, reliable, gorgeous but in a boring sort of way. Mark, frankly, was not a ballerina. Too clearly defined as a personality, insufficiently ingratiating, too self-engrossed. Izza was much better in the role. She floated around Tristan. He was her core, the pole to her banner, the peg to her blown-away tent. She appreciated him. She could make use of him.

Bronwen narrowed her eyes and smiled and sang and drummed on the biscuit-tin for them until they withdrew into the bracken, whereupon she put on her headphones and lay back. The afternoon passed.

Mark liked keeping an eye on people. Izza had been less startled by his proposal of marriage than she was by his request for her consent to his following her on the where-the-hell-are-you app. Tristan, of course, he'd been tracking for months. As soon as the Fair began to fall apart into a multitude of champagne-moments he checked his phone. What he saw made him smile. He texted both of them, 'Well done you found my favourite spot . . . hold on I'm coming'. Kurt dropped him home, and he took off westward on the Ducati. He was vain, he knew it, and vain enough to be amused by his own vanity. She probably thought he was a middle-aged smoothie. It would be fun, he thought, to roar into her life on the bike and carry her away in a whirl of black leather and hot metal. Tristan wouldn't mind, surely. He could pack up the picnic and bring the car back. He really seemed to like the car. Mark thought he might give it to him. Why? A sort of consolation prize.

Bronwen stood up and positioned herself so that Mark had to turn his back to the hollow full of bracken in order to greet her, but the respite that bought the hidden pair wasn't long.

'I was looking . . .' said Mark, nonplussed.

'Yeah. I came with Isolde,' said Bronwen.

The picnic things lay scattered. The empty bottles, the two glasses, the cherrystones that Izza had arranged in a triangle on a patch of bare ground as she talked.

'They went for a walk. Her and Tristan. I've been sleeping.'

The last statement was implausible. Bronwen was brisk as ever. Her irises had dwindled to pinpricks but you would still have trusted her to book a holiday for you, or to draw up a table-plan.

Mark dismounted ponderously. Roaring up is one thing, but you can't just swing down from the saddle of a bike and stride off. There's a lot of dragging and positioning to be done, and careful extending of the supporting leg. This other young woman needed to be absorbed into his planned future some-how – short-term only, he hoped. By the time his intended emerged from somewhere behind him, Tristan trailing her and doing that rather annoying thing with his thumb in his right ear, Mark was furious with himself for getting into this awkward situation. Why hadn't he waited at home and greeted Izza with poise intact, and a good bottle chilling in the fridge? He needed someone to kick. 'You've made a right mess, haven't you?' he said. 'This patch was pretty once, before you dropped all this crud around.'

Tristan, who knew what he was talking about, who had been trained up to Mark's extremely high standards of litter-awareness, began to pick up the plates. Izza came forward and put out her hands, taking his, and said, 'My life's partner!' in a high warbling voice. He thought, She's barking, and then, a moment later, She's off her face.

He got them all home in the car. The next day he sent Tristan to retrieve the bike from the Windsor police compound. It took all day and some acrimonious exchanges of opinion and lots of money. At least it got the boy out of Mark's hair while he accustomed himself to his bride.

Time passed. Love grew.

Mark's love for Izza, because he'd been right. He'd first seen her when she was dithering about in the centre of the Campo San Barnaba. She hadn't noticed him then, why should she, he was just another of the art-bods eating linguini with bottarga, one of the lucky ones who had got a table on the shady side opposite the church. He thought at once that she was fine and unusual and would need careful conservation work. He thought he would enjoy that. His companion knew who she was. Mark watched her. She looked tremulous and arrogant simultaneously, and the light reflected ripplingly off the canal accentuated her paleness as water brightens polished pebbles. Her hair was almost transparent. When the person she was waiting for arrived (in retrospect he realised it was Bronwen) she began to talk, to gush, not in the lazy colloquial sense of the word but like a spring after heavy rain. He saw that all her awkwardness, which was sexy in his eyes, came from the super-fluity of words in her and that once she had someone to talk to she found grace.

Then their mutual friend Morris fell off some scaffolding while squinting at a frescoed ceiling, and Mark and Izza were the only people in Venice who were prepared to help the poor guy. (Actually it was Bronwen who sorted out the insurance.) So they had each other's numbers, and they used them a lot. And then Mark made his reckless offer because he was bored of the life he had, and Tristan was proving hard to shake, and though they'd yet to have their first date he felt truly excited by her, as he had been by the Thracian cup – and look how well that had turned out. Once he'd got her, the sex was a pleasant surprise too – not because she was much of a performer but because her swooning disengagement from the process made him into one. He'd had women before, of course.

Tristan's love for Izza. That was delirium. Astonishing. Chemically-induced to start with, and chemically sustained, but only because it was so utterly fantastic when they took the tabs together that why wouldn't you keep doing it? Everything else faded out. Work, food, clubbing, clothes, movies, his thesis on the tension between the sacred and the secular in Renaissance depictions of the Virgin – all gone. It baffled him to remember how much time and energy he'd put into thinking about that stuff. All that was left was her – waiting for her, then being with her, then waiting until he could be with her again. In those waiting periods he was suspended, going through the motions, observing from very far away the manikin that was his everyday self, amazed at how trivial that banal self's occupations were – evenings prattling nonsense with his mates, mornings in the gallery smiling and suave, and let-me-know-if-you-need-any-help. And then, like the tide coming in with a rush, it would be time to see her again and he'd be right there, present, in his skin, every receptor alert, talking back when she talked to him (Christ how she talked!) kissing when she kissed him, dying, just totally dying of the bliss of it, when she dragged him into bed.

Bronwen's love for Izza. That was the strongest and truest. They all knew it. Bronwen couldn't abide compromise. Her mind was lucid, her thoughts consistent. Izza was the most important person for her, and so it would have been ridiculous for her not to devote herself entirely to Izza's care, Izza's happiness.

Mark accepted her. She was an asset to the gallery. It was so rare to find someone you could rely on absolutely. She instigated the practice whereby, each afternoon when he was in London, between three and five, he went through everything with her: every acquisition, every enquiry, every sale, every contact that needed following up, every piece of research that needed to be incorporated into an object's cataloguing. By the end of the afternoon he'd have made it through more work than he'd previously have done in a week, and felt light and free and joyful for it. As he left the gallery Bronwen would call

Izza and, though they never picked up, the lovers, recognising her ringtone, would haul themselves back from whatever circle of paradise they were in. When Mark got home, Tristan would be on the way out for the evening, waving to him from the basement steps (he'd moved down into the flat when the women arrived), and Izza would be upstairs, on the sofa in her study wearing spectacles, reading. Bronwen, watching over them from Cork Street, kept them all out of harm's way and by the time she came home, looking forward to a run and a shower and an arthouse movie delivered to her by MUBI, Izza and Mark would be out (so many openings to go to) or cooking together and she could congratulate herself on another day during which her darling had got away with it.

Mark's love for Tristan. That had always been a puny thing. No one missed it much.

Tristan's love for Mark. The funny thing about that was it was still flourishing. So much so that Tristan longed to tell Mark about his rapturous afternoons, just as he'd been used to telling him pretty well everything that passed through his mind. Knowing that they shared a woman made him feel tender towards his ex-lover. It was a bit of an odd emotion, he realised that, but jealousy wasn't any part of it. Whatever loving Izza felt like to Mark, it couldn't come near to resembling what was happening to Tristan. He was flying. He was melting. He was burning. He was expanding until he filled the sky and dwindling until he was a pill she could hold beneath her tongue. Mark didn't know how to cut loose. He was too good-looking ever to lose sight of himself. He couldn't possibly know what it was to feel any of this. Tristan felt sorry for him. He would like to have shared a little of his felicity, but he knew that would have been cruel. His silence was all he could offer as a token of his love. Or loving–kindness, more like, nowadays.

Izza's love. Who did Izza love? Did she love any of them? On the day of the wedding she had been luminous. It wasn't only the dress, the layer upon layer of sequinned grey chiffon, the floating sleeves, the skirts artfully tattered so that their diaphanous panels had no edges. That teary look, that made it seem she was never quite securely contained within her own skin, was more pronounced than ever. She walked in a miasma of glittering vapour, not that there was really a fog in the registry office. Beauty is as baffling as mist.

Mark, looking at her, saw treasure. Tristan saw a kind of nimbus into which he could fall and which would transport him, as golden painted clouds bear the Virgin up in depictions of the Assumption. Bronwen saw heartbreaking vulnerability. But Izza's glass-pale eyes showed no sign of seeing anyone – only the fixtures and fittings. She leant down to Mark and murmured to him about the ferociously varnished yellow pine benches, about the fitted carpet which crackled with static electricity, about the registrar's magenta lipstick. She was being funny, Mark realised that, but he was hurt. This was his life he was giving her. It wasn't a joke.

She was soft. She was fine as gossamer. But she was also somehow impervious. Was there even perhaps something wrong with her? He didn't really like to think this, but frankly wasn't it a bit odd the way she had agreed so readily to marry a stranger? As though actually she couldn't care less – as though she was so uninterested in anyone other than herself that any presentable man would do. 'Shut up,' he told himself. 'She's beautiful. She's the making of me. The new me. This is what I wanted. It's great, isn't it?' And, for a good long while, it was.

When Mark went to New York, as he fairly often did, or Dubai (he had a very loyal and appreciative client there), Izza began to drift into the gallery of a morning. She hadn't wanted to work there. It was essential to her, she told Mark, that her professional life should be independent of his. But despite all the people with whom she went for coffee – she had a well-filled address book – none of the encounters led to any job offers that she considered worth her while financially or helpful in terms of her personal development. So she was often in Cork Street. She'd be on her way to the London Library, where she might find inspiration for something or other. Or she'd be meeting someone for lunch so she might as well drop in first. Or it was raining, so whatever she'd planned was no-go. Tristan would look around and see her and it was as though the dove that comes rushing down the golden shaft of light to impregnate the Virgin of the Annunciation had tobogganed down into his heart. The sight of her filled him up, to bursting point, with joy.

They stood about together. Bronwen had a chair in her little back room but, while in the gallery, personnel were required to stay on their feet. They were absorbed in each other, but they were also very attentive to walk-ins. They didn't touch each other in public, or murmur endearments, or even look at each other too markedly, and their self-control generated a shimmering warmth. One visitor, after Izza had offered her fizzy water, and a hand-sheet, and had shown her the pre-Columbian crystal jaguar that seemed to pulse and emit sparks beneath the cunningly positioned laser-lights, put out a hand and said, 'What's happening to you, babe? Your aura's like off the graph!' and Tristan, hearing, thought, Yes. She's transfigured, isn't she? I didn't realise anyone else could see.

You know how this ends. Mark surprised them. It could have happened in any number of ways. Perhaps they were in the backroom, poring over a depiction of Lancelot and Guinevere, their shoulders touching, when he came in hours earlier than expected, having got fed up with the woman he'd been placed next to at the Met Gala dinner and taken a cab to JFK in time to make the red-eye. Perhaps Bronwen had a doctor's appointment (even Cerberus's eyes sometimes close) and wasn't there to hear Mark as he called from the doorway, 'I'm meeting Donatella for lunch in Le Bistro so I'll go straight on home after.' Perhaps he said to Izza one night, 'Is that a love-bite? You've not been doing it with Tristan have you?' (because he was familiar with Tristan's ways) and she, thinking he already knew everything, told him straight out.

It could have been any which way. The point is – he found out.

Nobody died. *Liebestod* is actually quite a rare occurrence. But Mark was taken aback to discover that, for all his sophistication, and for all his varied sexual history which might, you would have supposed, have made him immune to anything as dully conventional as jealousy, he deeply disliked the condition of cuckoldry. Was it because it was Tristan, who'd been his lover, and his protégé, and his kind of son? Not really. He'd never been possessive of the boy before – there were plenty of nights in the old days when they'd gone their separate ways.

He was astonished by how absolutely livid with rage he was at Izza's placidity. She never apologised. She moved around the Little Boltons, for days, packing up her preposterous quantity of gauzy dresses, talking serenely all the time about how love was a drug and an enchantment. She acted as if it was she and Tristan who were to be pitied when, as far as Mark could tell, they'd done exactly what they fucking well felt like without a moment's thought for anyone else. What a cow. Once he'd been delighted by the theatrical way she dressed. Now he thought 'blowsy'.

He didn't throw things or slam doors. He didn't cry. He didn't let himself down. The only person he yelled at was Bronwen because in stories like this it's never the perpetrators who seem loathsome, only the enablers who haven't, poor things, had even so much as a nibble of the forbidden fruit.

The two women moved to Lisbon. Bronwen became a highly successful dealer in pre-Isabelline Iberian ceramics. Mark told people she'd picked up all she knew from him, but when he was being honest with himself (which he usually was – it's what made him so quick and flexible as a businessman) he knew how much she'd taught him too. The gallery was much better run thanks to her systems. Izza became, in sequence, a junkie, a psychotherapist, a condessa, and then, to everyone's surprise, a nun.

*   *   *

Time passed. Love, and its attendant jealousies and resentments, dwindled to a manageable size.

Mark and Tristan met in Kensington Gardens. They hadn't seen each other for nearly a decade. Although there was a fifteen-year age gap between them they had arrived simultaneously at an appreciation of the pleasures of middle age: gardening, Schubert, dogs. Mark had a rough-haired Pointer (female), Tristan an Airedale (male).

The dogs sniffed each other's backsides and at once they were deeply, ecstatically, helplessly in love. Their human companions stood watching them while they twirled and pounded the earth, celebrating the wonder that was the other, and the miraculous good fortune that had brought them together. The pointer performed clumsy earth-bound pirouettes. The terrier leapt up and down on the spot, yapping.

'Is this what it was like for Bronwen, do you suppose?' asked Tristan.

'Watching the two of us, you mean?'

'Being driven crazy by her. Yes.'

'So,' said Mark. 'You're suggesting that Bronwen stood in relation to Isolde as you and I do to Biscuit and . . . what's yours called?'

'Willesden.'

'Good name. That's where you live?'

'Yes.'

'With?'

'You're asking am I available?'

'Dearest Tristan, no. No. I'm not. I'm not asking that. I'm a married man.'

'Yeah. I was at the wedding, remember. I handed you the rings.'

'And very lovely you looked. How could I forget? But no. Not that marriage. He's called Brian. You?'

'The love potion worked for me. No one else has come close. I think about her every day. I was with someone for a while. Guess what. She was called Izza, short for Isabella. Not exactly moving on.'

'Another woman?'

'Yes. That stuck too.'

'Why did you let her go, then?'

Tristan looked out over the Round Pond. It was a late afternoon in September. The light was piercingly beautiful, silver-gilt and icy clear and loaded with the melancholy of summer's passing and the irrecoverability of lost time. The dogs were now performing a pas de deux which involved Willesden's lying flat to the ground, barking, while Biscuit made repeated lunge-and-retreat moves. 'Shall we walk?' he said.

And so they walked and they talked and by the time they had passed under the bridge into Hyde Park, and called the dogs off when they tried to steal bread-crusts from a Japanese family who were feeding the ducks, and scoffed at the Diana fountain, and remembered the time they got locked into the park after an opening at the Serpentine Gallery and took off all their clothes and swam together, and kissed very carefully because they really really hadn't wanted to swallow any of that soupy brown water, they were fond friends again.

'What happened?' said Mark. 'Why haven't we seen each other all these years?'

'Because I adored you and you dumped me. Because you're a heartless bastard. And because then I betrayed you,' said Tristan, but he wasn't very interested in that question. Instead he reverted to the earlier one. He said, 'I think part of the reason I didn't go after her was that she didn't ask me to. But I can see now that was absurd. I was supposed to be the wooer. I wasn't very confident back then. But also . . . She wasn't the kind of person you could run off with. Insubstantial. Do you remember telling me off for making her up?'

'No. What did I mean by that?'

'You've forgotten all about me, haven't you?' Now Tristan sounded really hurt. 'It was a thing we did. I'd tell you silly stories about the people we met. It was fun. We didn't really have that much to talk about so . . . Well. It was a private thing we had.'

Mark said, 'And so?'

'I still do it,' said Tristan. 'I teach. All the kids love stories.'

'Great. But . . .'

'What I mean is you were right. We both made her up. You more than me. You invented a woman you could marry. And I invented one who could whisk me up to heaven. You said she was real, but that wasn't actually true.'

Mark considered. His memories of that time were full of hectic colour and jittery excitement. It was when the dealership was really getting going. It was while he was with Izza that he had made his first sale to the British Museum. He remembered coming back from meetings, strung to the maximum tension with adrenalin. He remembered how her languor and her tallness had turned him on. He remembered very exactly how he had felt about her archaic vocabulary and the slow way she drew out her complex sentences, how he'd relished it as he relished the virtuosity of a glass-blower or, for that matter, of a football team playing perfectly in concert. He remembered her scent. He remembered how naked she seemed, far more so than any of the other people with whom he'd been to bed. The softness of her thighs. The blueness of her veins. She'd seemed pretty real to him.

'Now you're making things up again,' he said.

'Probably,' said Tristan. 'That's what lovers do.'

PIPER

He kept the bus parked on the old airstrip, between the remains of a hangar and a couple of abandoned horse trailers. That way, he thought, if one of the tricky winds that sometimes came off the sea hurtled through, the old lady would be propped both sides. A double-decker is an unstable thing. A wonder really that Hyde Park Corner wasn't heaped up with toppled red carcasses. Perhaps people in London drove very slow. He supposed they must. He couldn't say. He'd never been.

The bus was his home, but for his daily back-and-forth he used the transit. Powder-blue, but then he'd got the kiddies to jazz it up for him. A spring day, and he'd gone into Franklin's and the two girls were teetering about in those skirts that were more like socks really – knitted, tight – and he'd said, 'What are you doing with that lot?' A great pile of aerosols, gold and silver and red and green.

'They won't be needed again 'til next Christmas,' said the one with the long black-painted nails. 'We've got to put out the seed potatoes now, and the potted daffs.'

He said, 'I'll take them off your hands.'

She said, 'What, all of them?' and her friend sniggered. Or perhaps they weren't friends. He thought about it sometimes. About what it must be like to do a job that kept you every day in the same place. Suppose there was someone there who drove you round the twist? A nightmare that would be, a real nightmare.

The girls let him have the spray-paint cheap because someone had come in on Christmas Eve, that's what they said, and complained about how one of the nozzles was all gummed up. 'It's like aeons they've been here,' said the other one, the smiler. 'Anyway, when did you last see anyone spray-paint a teasel?'

'My mum still does it, every year,' said black-nails, but Piper was already shovelling the shiny cylinders into his big bag. 'Fiver for the lot,' he said, and they let him take them.

Come Sunday he had the whole of the junior school out at the airstrip. He made overalls for them out of cement bags and he told them he wanted the van to look like a birthday present, so when they'd painted every inch of it they got a roll of silver foil out of the bus (he kept his kitchen neat as could be – everything put away in the little drawers he'd fixed up) and they made a big silver bow and fixed it to the bonnet. He took off his shirt then (it was one of his good ones) and stood there in his old combats and gave the two littlest ones the last two cans of paint – green for the deaf boy who chirruped as he talked, red for that girl who was so tiny he wondered was she all right, or what. They each painted one leg, and half his bum, and then they started on his bare chest and he didn't want to spoil the day by yelling at them. Took hours, it did, to get it off his chest hair and the scrubbing with white spirit gave him a rash.

The mothers complained about that too, and the next day Sylvia from Shortcuts called after him down the street, 'Thanks for the business, Piper. I've been cutting sparkly hair non-stop since school came out.' They went for a drink and he showed her his golden belly button. The chirruping boy was hers. All the mums were glad of a morning's peace when he took the kiddies off their hands.

This time of year it was all rats. Late August, September, he'd be running all over the county with his wasp gear. Mice, of course, that was pretty constant, though he used to say to them all, 'You don't need me. Get a cat.' He wasn't a pushy salesman – didn't need to be.

When he was only a squit of a thing he'd made his Ma a mouse out of half a hazelnut shell. He drew on eyes and whiskers with her eyeliner, and glued on a bit of string for a tail. Sweet, it was, with its pointy nose. Some of the mice he poisoned were that small. It bothered him, really, that people couldn't live and let live, but you can't be an exterminator if you're going to get upset. People don't like mouse pellets in their bread bins. They just don't. You can't blame them. He knew all about bubonic plague. Not that you're likely to pick that up in Suffolk.

It was a substantial town. The market square was broad and entirely enclosed by buildings, not one of which was less than a hundred and sixty years old. A lych-gate opened on to the churchyard, which was rectangular and amply large enough to contain all the smug and boastful tombstones that had been erected there by generation upon generation of townsfolk, proud of their families' long continuance in this place. Even the semis flanking the London road were, by modern standards anyway, solidly built.

Piper knew, though, on what an insecure and permeable base this handsome assemblage of shops and pubs and houses had been founded. It was not immediately evident to a visitor – because the river ran beneath the Thoroughfare through a subterranean channel, and because the bridges carrying walkers from one river bank to another traversed only the side-alleys – that this was a town suspended above water and air, above a system of tubular vessels as complex as those which conduct blood to the extremity of a limb. A town should rest on solid matter, if it is to be safe from alarums, but this one stood on a bed of liquid, dark river-water, and of gas, the dank air of underground.

Such tunnels are unattractive to human beings. The engineers who descended there periodically to dredge out the silt and to clear the points of ingress from the sewers, and the egress to the river downstream, went doggedly, and only because such work is well remunerated. For Piper's antagonists, though, the vaults and undercrofts beneath the town constituted an entirely congenial habitat – moist, dark, rich in nutritional foodstuffs both animate and decayed. They liked the privacy, and the easy access, by drainpipe mostly, to the houses raised above them. Piper's services would never cease to be required.

*   *   *

Sylvia always allowed plenty of time for breakfast because her little boy would get agitated, and then he couldn't get his porridge down. She read aloud to him to keep everything calm, and he would gaze at her.

He was very intelligent. She knew that, even if nobody else did. But when he fixed his eyes on her as she read there was something a bit spooky about it. He sucked the words from her lips into his mind. She read the sort of stories children his age like, about furry animals, and sometimes he would move his hand very gently about three inches above the tabletop as though he was stroking a guinea pig.

Sometimes she thought she loved him so much she would explode. When there was a man, when you felt that strongly about a grown man, then you knew what to do about it, though he wouldn't always be interested. But loving children didn't have an outcome like that. All you could do was stare and stare at them and sometimes it made her want to cry. She would stop and mime eating and he would look bewildered but then slowly he would lift his spoon and she would carry on.

The porridge was delicious. She put honey in it, and apple stewed with cloves. It was their favourite food. When the boy's father was still living with them they didn't have it so often. So his leaving wasn't all bad, she supposed.

One morning she looked up from the page and Billy's eyes weren't on her. That was unusual. He was looking at something near her elbow. She looked too, and there was a rat. Its teeth were yellow. She was terrified. She didn't know how it could have got up on to the table and at once it seemed to her she could feel things climbing up her legs, scrambling over her shoulders, crossing her lap.

She stood up and the rat looked over its shoulder and was gone. She saw it whisk into the space under the kitchen sink. The boy began to cry, and so did she. He said 'Ratty', and she made herself smile at him, but she took away his porridge unfinished and got him into his coat and hurried him along to the school as fast as she could go without running.

All that morning Piper worked flat-out. He had to lug his stuff from one end of the Thoroughfare to another. He had a word with the woman in the estate agent who kept an eye on the parking when Mr Plod wasn't in town and she said, 'All right, just for once, but don't block the view of my window display.'

He stopped up pipes. He re-fixed skirting boards. He put wire mesh over fireplaces and piled bricks on top of trapdoors. He gave instructions about the protection of family pets. In each house he left half a dozen saucers full of pretty powder-blue pellets. He said, 'It's unlikely you'll find them dead. They take themselves off. And it's more than unlikely you'll find them alive now I've been through. That doesn't happen.' He was wearing his red and green trousers. The paint made them rather stiff, but waterproof, and he wore them all the time for work now. When the mothers noticed them they smiled at him.

The next day there were no rats to be seen, and Piper was able to get on with some maintenance around the bus. He reckoned he could. He'd done so well the day before. Not that everyone had paid up right away, but he'd go easy on the ones who were waiting for their benefits. Some of the men said he got paid a different way. He ignored the talk. Half of the women in town were collecting their pensions, for Christ's sake. He kept it professional, always, but he did think a bit about Sylvia now that that fellow was gone. Her house smelled of something warm and sharp that reminded him of home.

Anyway he'd filled up on petrol and paid Mike at the garage what he owed him and closed his tab at the Bull. Rats were his enemies, but where, he thought, would he be without them? Up shit creek without a paddle.

On the third day the woman who came in from the county town to teach the big ones computer skills arrived early, as she always did because it took her a while to set up. She went into the larger of the two classrooms, and put on the light and the floor reared up and came towards her and flowed across her feet and on into the corridor. She screamed until she had no more breath and then she fainted and when she came to she was on the ground and there were things tangled in her hair, things scrabbling and tugging at it, and a sour, repulsive smell.

The parents waiting outside could hear her. Some of them made calls on their mobiles. They couldn't guess what was going on. Then they saw the double doors open, as they always did around this time of the morning. The terracotta plaques said G for girls on the left, B for boys on the right, though of course the children all went in together nowadays. Miss Ellie had a theatrical way of flinging the doors wide to announce the start of the morning. This time, though, they seemed to bulge, and then yield. It was like a birth, and what was born was legion, horrible, and very fast.

Parents picked up their littlest ones and ran with them, shouting to the bigger boys and girls to follow. They slammed their doors shut behind them, those who lived in town, and ran upstairs. The farming families got in their cars and sat – adults quivering, children sobbing – like sailors on an eel-infested sea. The tarmac was seething. There was a high-pitched chattering, and always that smell.

The ones with phones stopped dialling 999. They weren't getting through anyway. They all called Piper.

He was clearing the brambles round the back of the hangar. He fancied setting up a sort of workshop there. He'd been thinking about that hazelnut mouse and it had got some ideas flowing. The holidaymakers who rented cottages nearer the coast in August, they were always looking for little somethings to take home. He could rent one of the tar-paper shacks the fishermen didn't use any more – might get one for free actually. The Mouse House, he'd call it. He could get a whole load of those sugar mice his mother used to put in his stocking. Cards. He'd make biscuits. Gingerbread mice. Mice made out of seashells. He'd always fancied himself as a woodcarver. He could make whole families of them. He imagined a mother mouse in an apron and father with a beret. Soft toys too. Sylvia – she made her own clothes. Must have lots of scraps. It's a pretty easy shape to cut out. A kind of partnership.

Hold on there. Keep it professional.

In the bus, while he hummed to himself over the racket of the strimmer, his phone rang and rang and rang.

*   *   *

The streets were deserted. All the shops had closed, those that had opened at all. At least twice a year, when there'd been heavy rain upriver, water seeped up through the cobbles of the Thoroughfare, turning back gardens into bogs, and making the lino on kitchen floors squelch underfoot. Most of the families had sandbags about, just in case. Now people had jammed them against the inside of their front doors – not the right way to do it, but no one wanted to let anything in. No one opened a window. If the rats could climb up the slick slippery interiors of the drainage pipes it would be no trouble for them to hoist themselves up a perpendicular brick wall. People heard scurrying on the roof tiles, and rammed chests of drawers across chimney breasts. A child came screaming out of a bathroom and her mother slammed the toilet seat down, just in time, on a wet dark thing.

Piper drove into town at last. He took his gaudy van, all decked out in the colours of fire and fir-trees, right into the Thoroughfare again, weaving sedately between the bollards designed to exclude cars. He switched off the engine, and sat watching. He knew how many human eyes must be on him. His phone kept buzzing as the messages stacked up. He took no notice. He watched the rats. He'd heard about this sort of infestation but never thought he'd see it.

In normal circumstances rats are selfish, non-cooperative creatures. They are hangers-on of the human race, but by humans they are detested and shunned and chased with pitch-forks. The emotional atmosphere in which they have evolved has not favoured the development of altruism. They look for food and when they find it they eat it fast and furtively, always on the lookout for competitors of their own kind. They have no partners. They don't care for the pack. They don't even care for their families. In certain circumstances, though, they band together, and when they do so their unanimity is absolute.

Piper ate a cheese sandwich he'd made for himself before setting out. He didn't think he was going to get much of a break once his day's work had begun. By the time he'd finished, and licked the chutney off his fingers, his van had grown a thick carapace of furred bodies.

He heard the scuffling and scuttling all around him. He heard the tiny screech of clawed feet skidding down the van's sides. Pale bellies pressed themselves against the windscreen. Bent-pin claws fixed themselves to the wipers. When he saw them beginning to gnaw at the edges of the bonnet – they wanted to have a go at the rubber seal – he started up the engine. They froze. He reversed, and they began to drop off. He jerked into first gear and gunned the engine. As he drove away rats flew out behind him.

'Where's he going, Mummy?' chirped Sylvia's little boy, huddled next to her in the loft and peeping through an air-vent. 'Isn't he going to save us? If Piper can't save us, what will we do?'

The river that crept beneath the town surfaced beyond it. For the last part of its course it meandered, as rivers should, open to the sky. Ponderous ginger-haired cattle grazed the water-meadows to each side of it. At this season the bulrushes were last year's – black and rebarbative – but the wild garlic was up, stinking fresh, and there were tiny blue and white anemones starring the grass under the willow trees.

Piper took the old road that ran along the river valley, the one with grass growing along the spine of the tarmac like the coarse black hairline on a donkey's back. He hummed as he drove. His eyes were narrowed to slits. He was planning his route. He had to have a clear run to the sea. The tide was propitious. He talked to himself silently, in the way he often did, soundlessly but with his lips moving, and he looked extremely pleased with what he had to say.

At the airstrip he moved fast and methodically. He'd made the bus's top deck cosy, with a proper bed spanning the entire width at the back, and benches built in. He kept it neat. The lower deck was where he stacked his gear. He trundled out the great black coffin-sized boxes, the coils of rubber-coated cable, the silvery metal containers that rattled as he loaded them up.

He was a long time inside the transit, clipping this to that and stapling that to the other thing. He checked his tyres and topped up the radiator and the reservoir of windscreen-washing fluid. He climbed up onto the roof of the van and secured the superstructure he needed, the gangling metal assemblage of bars and saucers and needle-thin antennae. He changed into his black biking clobber (it still fitted, even though it was seven years since he'd got rid of the Harley). The boots rang against the metal floor of the bus. He put his particoloured trousers back on over the leathers. He gelled his hair and shaved his face, carrying the enamel basin of boiled water out into the sunshine and using his old ivory-handled brush and the wooden dish of cedarwood soap.

On going into battle, he'd been told, the Spartan warriors made themselves as sleek as oiled blades. It was a practice he approved of.

He made sure that the transit's every door and window was closed up tight, and he set off back into town.

Sylvia and her boy were in the bathroom. She had a vague idea that rats couldn't swim so they might be safest there, although the old thing about sinking ships bothered her. Anyway bathtime was always soothing, and Billy was content. His fingertips were dead-white and wrinkled as walnut kernels, and normally she would have got him out hours ago, but today wasn't normal and it was a relief when he stopped fretting and started on a long story about his shoal of rubber fishes, muttering sometimes to her but mostly to himself. She sat on the wicker chair and let her mind go blank.

There were dark shapes swinging and bumping against the windows, but thank goodness it was impossible to distinguish, through the frosted glass, whether they were moving leaves (as though there were leaves that size this early) or something else. After all, she'd never, she thought, heard of anyone actually being killed by rats.

The tiny girl, who never seemed to grow, was with her dad, who saw to her on a Thursday when his wife had to go for her treatment. The girl wasn't afraid, though he was. She clambered onto the back of the sofa that was pushed up against the front window so that she could watch the way the rat horde surged over the cobbles, or mounted the raised flower beds like cresting waves, ebbing back down again to leave nothing but scrabbled grey earth where the tulips and forget-me-nots had been.

She was very attentive and curious. Are they hungry? she asked. Do they have homes? Will they get tired soon? Are mice baby rats or are they different? Why have they come? I don't know said her father. I expect so. I'm not sure. No – mice are different. I wish they never bloody well had.

Piper parked at the point where the Thoroughfare debouched into the market square. He sat still for a bit, calculating angles.

He'd had a disco when he was still at school. He'd built the rig himself, and made a packet going around the big houses where the kids who went to day-schools in London had their eighteenths. The bigger the house, the less time the owners spent in it. It didn't make him indignant, the way it did some of the men who drank in the pub. People interested him, the illogical ways they did things. He didn't get angry with them, any more than he got angry with rats.

The disco gave him power. If he spotted a lad with that yearning look that made a face lose definition and go kind of mushy, he'd lend a hand by putting on the Walker Brothers and next time the boy shuffled past him he'd have his cheek sweatily clamped to his girl's and his hand in her hair.

Piper could swivel the speakers from inside the van. He did a neat five-point turn, minutely adjusting the direction of his front wheels so he was ready for the off. He was hesitating between the *Ode to Joy* and *The Blue Danube*. Rats, he'd found, responded to pretty much the same repertoire as the middle-brow, middle-aged human. Then he thought, no, let's sock it to them, and he put on the march from *The Pirates of Penzance*.

Baah Baah Bababa Baah. The masses of grey bodies that had twitched and undulated ceaselessly all morning across the paving of the market square stilled. Innumerable torpedo-pointed heads turned in the direction of the van.

Bah bababa baba. Bah bababa baba. The roofs shed their loads. Tiny clawed feet skittered and scrabbled their way down sheer concrete, down usefully cratered terracotta brick, down lumpen pebble-dash with its helpful protuberances. As the upper levels of the town cleared, the ground became ever more densely packed with shuffling bodies.

Baah Baah. Piper turned his key in the ignition. Bababa Baah. As the speakers picked up the power generated by the engine the volume surged mightily. Bah bababa baba. The pilastered front of the neo-Grecian town hall, the blackened timbers of the Corn Exchange, the symmetrical sash windows of the row of Georgian merchant's houses, all gave back the sound, superbly resonant.

Tiny Elsa got down from the sofa-back, crying, and her father picked her up and snuggled her under his armpit so that her ears were comfortingly blocked by T-shirted flesh. Sylvia and her boy thumped down the stairs on their bottoms, which was Billy's favourite way of descending, and felt to her, in this time of weird menaces, like a sensible precaution against God-knows-what.

The Venetian blinds rattled against the glass at the front of the house. At the back there was a sound of incessant soft thumping on the flat roof of the kitchen, as though it was hailing slippers.

*   *   *

Piper took it slow. His followers' legs averaged less than a centimetre in length. They could scurry pretty quick considering, but still. To maintain the momentum he had to keep them in his force field. In first gear the transit groaned and bunny-hopped. In second, at that pace, it repeatedly stalled. Each time it did, the music stuttered and the volume level dropped, but the rats, it turned out, weren't bothered. The D'Oyly Carte company's performance, as transmitted by Piper's makeshift sound-system, might jerk and hiccup, but the river of rat-flesh flowed, smooth and collected as a spill of mercury, down the Thoroughfare and across the mini-roundabout. (Piper's van went around it but his mud-grey velvet train swirled straight across, devouring somehow, without pausing or deviating, all the pansies forming the floral clock.) Slowly, slowly, out along Quay Street with more rats dropping silently from window ledges or pouring like slurry down the embankment beneath the railway line to join the flood.

The windows were full of faces. Piper didn't look up at them. He'd be the hero of the hour, but he didn't kid himself that he would be liked for it. He looked odd, with his beaky nose and his flaming hair. His arms were unusually long and he'd heard some of the kids call him monkey-man. But it's not as though all the men who walked into the pub to cries of 'what are you having' and 'over here' were that easy on the eye either. It wasn't any deficiency in the looks department that made Piper an object of suspicion – other way round, if anything. The men had a nasty feeling he was attractive to women, though they themselves couldn't see it. It was more to do with his not living in a house, not working alongside anyone else, not being from thereabouts.

On the way out of town there was a house that looked like a castle. The brewer who built it, some hundred years earlier, had had a fanciful side. He liked his wife to wear velvet and do up her hair in a snood dotted with artificial pearls. His daughters were called Deirdre and Genevieve. He liked the words 'bosky', 'crenellation', and 'casement'. The river ran along the bottom of his garden. He had an engraving of the drowning Ophelia above the big black sideboard where three different types of sherry sat, in decanters heavy enough to brain a burglar with, on an elaborately scrolled silver tray.

By the time Deirdre died there, after seventy-five years of scatter-brained spinsterhood (Genevieve had married and gone to live in Canada), the garden had become very pretty. Willows grew aslant. Tiny pink and white roses rambled through the old apple trees. No one cut the asparagus any more – Deirdre didn't like getting her fingers buttery – but in June its pale green plumes waved, feeble and lovely, over the flagged paths.

Once she was gone, though, the new proprietor got the place sorted out.

Humphrey Leach was a realist. His words were 'tidy', 'low-maintenance' and 'cost-effective'. Now the castle rose from an expanse of grey gravel and there were spiky succulents in square concrete containers by the bolted door. The willows had been pollarded and the river embanked, and there was a long fibreglass thing, halfway between a surfboard and canoe, on which Humphrey Leach liked to skim up and down the river, wearing tight clothes purpose-made for practitioners of his preferred mode of high-speed punting. His girlfriend was extremely thin.

Piper's van crawled by. His entourage now trailed behind him for nearly quarter of a mile, a squeaking mass of entranced rodents. They jostled and snapped at each other. Baaah Baaah baba bah bah. Outliers trampled the crocuses on the verges alongside the new-built semis. Breakaway parties mounted walls garlanded with aubretia and ran along their crests, barging each other aside.

Baah baba ba baba. Piper was singing along. In his wing mirror he could see Jenny Leach from year five scrambling over the castle's electronic gates. She was a nice kid. He hadn't realised she was Humphrey's daughter. Hadn't put the names together in his head. That scraggy woman was surely never her mother. He'd seen to a wasps' nest for them once. He was there for a good three quarters of an hour and all that while Humphrey and the woman were doing press-ups on the lawn. They had earphones in. No conversation. Just grunting. Can't be much fun for the girl. He'd take her along with the other big ones when it came to blackberrying time.

The stretch of coastline to the east of the town was curiously formed. The sea was only five miles away, as the crow flies, but the river travelled closer to twelve to reach it. It ambled from side to side of the broad water-meadows, filling the whole shallow valley with its silt. Cows stood knee-deep on its verges and swans drifted above its mud. It had its own landscape of kingcups and dragonflies, willows and bog-grass. It wasn't in a hurry to be swallowed up in the brown undifferentiating sea.

When the meadows gave way to salty marshland where samphire grew and little birds with long legs and beaks strutted, the river did a sudden swerve. A shingle bank had arisen over the centuries to protect it, a miles-long finger of shifting stony ground wide enough for a road of sorts, and fishermen's tarred shacks, and the forbidding rubble of past wars.

You could drive out along that bank. Lots of people did. You could tell that by the numbers of bottles scattered about the Martello tower and the stench of urine in the Second World War pillboxes. On one side lay the sea, heaving. On the other side, considerably lower at this phase of the tide, ran the river. Along that road going nowhere, Piper went, and the rats followed him. Me too, I'm coming, they might have been chattering. Keep up keep up keep up keep up. They were exhausted, and hungry.

Baah baah baba ba bah. Piper kept an eye on the flow. He'd known this river since he was a boy chucking flat stones at it. He could see, by the way it dimpled, in which direction the current was running. He was satisfied. When he got to the steep dip where last year's spring tides had burst through the shingle, he left the track and took the van very slowly down the landward side on to the marshy expanse alongside the river. He drove in a big circle so that the rats following him swirled together. The music never let up. He wouldn't be wanting to listen to that tune again any time soon. He was watching the break in the sea wall, that notch. He could see spray beyond it. There was an alteration in the light, an increase in the volume of sound coming from the sea. He turned the van carefully. He knew exactly the course he'd have to take, and he knew he'd have to go like the clappers.

When the tide broke roaring through, he was ready. The Pirates' chorus snapped off, and he was racing along the overgrown causeway, kicking up spray, feeling his wheels skidding under the pressure of water weighted and solidified by the bodies of a million drowning rodents. On the further side of the breach, when he reckoned he was high enough, he switched off the engine and got out his second cheese sandwich. There was no way he'd get the transit back over the marshes until the tide had receded. He watched the mass of struggling rats being carried upriver a way, and there being whirled around by the tricky currents where the incoming tide met the outgoing flood of the river, and then being tossed and churned again as they were tumbled back past him and on out to sea. Will the seagulls eat them, he wondered? Or do they think rats are dirty too?

The following morning, once he'd shaved, and once he'd hosed down the transit, he drove into town and went to the estate agents' office, where he knew he'd find Humphrey Leach, and he presented his bill.

It was a surprising fact about the town that it was a communist enclave. There'd been a long shop there once, where they made engines and farm machinery. And there was a charismatic journeyman who'd drifted there from the Welsh valleys a hundred years ago – he was Silvia's great-grandfather – and made himself quite a reputation by singing nightly in the pub before he signed up at the shop, and began making trouble there, as the proprietor put it, or rather, as the other workmen saw it, teaching them to stand up for their rights. The pity of it was that, whether or not a decent wage was a human right, the proprietor couldn't pay it and keep the business in profit, so the agitation ended with the closing of the works, and the men drifting off to Lowestoft and Folkestone, looking to make their livings on the docks there. But the Welshman stayed, and became the town's barber, and made a go of it because men loved the way he sang as he soaped their cheeks, and it was under his influence that the town council veered leftward. They stopped calling themselves the Soviet of East Suffolk after the invasion of Hungary, but they still sang the 'Internationale' and the 'Marseillaise' and they kept on conducting their meetings on the Leninist model.

By the time Piper came to town their revolutionary rhetoric had become a quaint tradition. They addressed each other as 'comrade', rather as the old codger who kept the key of the Dissenters' Chapel made a point of calling visitors 'Brother' or 'Sister'. Funny how conservatism can be a preserver of the revolution. The Chapel was their meeting place. Its layout was supposed to undermine the oppressive authority of Almighty God. No altar. But where the altar might have been there was a lofty pulpit, or crow's nest (the roof timbers all came from wrecked ships) from which a preacher could survey and domi-nate the gathering.

Sylvia didn't usually go along, but she'd heard her customers chattering all morning about Piper's demands. Outrageous, they said. Who does he think he is? Well, who is he, actually? It's a bit weird, isn't it, the way he hangs around the school. Has he ever had a girlfriend here, do you know? Sylvia buttoned her lip, but after tea she dropped Billy round at Little Elsa's place. Elsa's mum was lying down but the two children didn't need entertaining when they had their Sylvanian Families to play with.

Down at the chapel they were at it full tilt.

Man 1 *(pedantic, soft-spoken, keeps making notes in a little black book)* – What we need to ascertain is precisely who took it upon themselves to employ Mr Piper.

Woman 1 *(she was the one who always brought the yappy little dog into the café at elevenses time, however often the waitress asked her not to)* – You're not going to be able to pin that on anyone in particular. There wasn't a phone in town that wasn't ringing his number.

Woman 2 *(Miss Ellie from the school)* – I think we have to accept collective responsibility, don't we?

Woman 3 – I mean really we were all begging him, weren't we? We'd have paid anything. I had such nightmares last night you wouldn't believe. Slugs it was, slugs all over.

Man 2 *(he had a JCB digger, and he'd been the first man in town to wear an earring)* – Remember the frogs, Gina? You dreamt a lot about them, too, didn't you?

Woman 3 blushes. People look at her curiously. They hadn't known those two had had a thing. Or was Man 2 just having them on? He was such a cocksure bastard. He'd have liked to have been the one who saw off the rats. He was jealous. You could tell.

The door opened and Humphrey Leach came in. He climbed straight up into the pulpit. No one had ever sat there before. He said 'Let's get started' as though nothing said before he graced them with his presence could possibly be of any account. His thin woman sat down on one of the benches, with the girl beside her. Humphrey had called his daughter Jennifer – a name he considered unexceptionable and fit-for-purpose. She thought of herself as Jasmine. Her friends called her Jazz.

Sylvia was on the bench opposite. She gave Jazz a smile. She'd promised the girl Saturday work shampooing, once exams were over.

Humphrey Leach read out the invoice from top to bottom. He managed to convey incredulity at every word, from the sender's address 'The Bus, Elmswood Airfield' to the directions for payment 'Cash only'. The bill was meticulously detailed. So much for use of equipment. So much for petrol consumed. So much for subsistence (the two cheese sandwiches). So much (and yes – it was so, so, so very much) for services of expert pest-controller, as charged by the hour @ a rate that made most of those present assume they must have misheard.

Sylvia *(silently to herself)* – He'll never get that. What's he playing at?

Man 1 – We have been debating, Mr Leach, should this be viewed as a charge on the town as a collective entity?

Humphrey Leach – You bet your life it should. You're not suggesting I should pay it, are you?

Nobody had been suggesting that, not for one moment. But now they thought, Well you could, couldn't you? And none of the rest of us can.

They liked Piper on the whole. They thought he was good with the kiddies, and no, no one thought there was anything weird about the way a single man in his thirties liked having them around. Or if anyone did wonder about it they weren't saying so yet.

Man 3 – There's a lot of damage to be made good. And I'd say we ought to get the sewers sluiced through with DDT.

More voices –

Every single car-tyre. Every car parked in town. They ate the lot.

Those trees. We planted them for the Jubilee. My mum . . . she was ninety then . . . she dug the first hole.

She was a fine lady, your mum. Used to make the best lemon curd.

I've always liked the *Mikado*.

It wasn't the *Mikado*, Dad, it was that other one.

Did you see how they went at the veg outside Mr Bailey's? Not a leaf left. Not a stalk.

There's going to be quite a few have to shut up shop.

And no one to pay compensation.

Did he say conversation.

No, darling. Compensation.

Woman 3 (*she has recovered her composure*) – I thought he was doing it as a favour. I mean being neighbourly. You know. Because he was the one who knew what to do. Like you'd do, you know, if there was a fire or something. You wouldn't ask for money after, would you.

Man 2 (*he drinks with Piper sometimes – not that Piper comes to the pub much*) – That's a hell of a lot of equipment he's got. I mean it's not just turning on a hose, is it?

Man 3 *(he's a reliable brickie. There's contractors from Woodbridge to Beccles who call on him when they've got a lot of work on)* – And it's not like he is a neighbour, really, is it? I mean he's not from here.

> Medley of voices –
> Not far off. His dad had the garage in Wangford.
> No, that was Porter, wasn't it?
> Bob Porter. That man could whistle any tune in the
>   hymnbook.
> Never went to church though, did he?
> Wouldn't have wanted God looking into his conscience,
>   I reckon. He was never short of a pheasant or two for
>   his dinner, was he?
> Could fix a trap as neat as he could fix a carburettor.
> Anyway . . .
> But Piper, he wasn't anything to do with old Bob
>   Porter.
> Where's he from then?
> Been around for years, hasn't he? I remember him with
>   all the other lads kicking a ball about down the
>   water-meadows.
> He wasn't at the school though, was he?
> Would have been about my age. No, he wasn't there.
> He doesn't come to the pub much.
> It'd give you the shivers a bit, wouldn't it, thinking of all
>   that poison he handles.
> Was he evacuated or something? Like in the war.
> I don't know any Pipers. It's not a Suffolk-sounding
>   name.

Not sure it's his surname even. It could be, like, a
nickname sort of thing.
I mean. He can't have just dropped from the sky,

And yet, for all anybody knew, it seemed as though he had.

There were eight of the littleys from year two sitting on the top
deck of Piper's bus. They liked to pretend the bus was going
somewhere. As they sat down, their jelly-shoes swinging and
the prickly stuff of the seats chafing their dimpled thighs,
Piper said, 'So where are we off to today?'

Often they said 'Seaside!' Sometimes they said 'Timbuctoo'.
Sometimes they said 'Fairyland!' This time they said, 'Into the
mountain.' 'Not yet,' said Piper, 'We'll only go there if the
worst comes to the worst. Would Over-the-Rainbow do you?'
and he got out his rainbow banner and hung it from the ceiling and they all squealed and giggled and when he'd given out
the pink wafer biscuits they settled down to cutting mouse
shapes out of fuzzy felt.

Piper sat on his bed and started to clean his saxophone.

'Piper,' said tiny Elsa. 'Will you be playing with my daddy
at the Big Gig?'

'I haven't decided yet,' he said. 'That depends.'

Miss Ellie asked Jennifer Leach to come along with her to pick
up the littleys. She wanted to have a word with the girl but she
didn't want to make it sound too important so she just said,
'I'm going Wenhaston way. Anyone want a lift home?' She

knew Jazz was the only one in the class who lived in that direction.

In the minibus she was trying out openings in her head . . . 'So, Jennifer, how do you feel about boarding school? . . . Jennifer, if you'd like me to have a word with your father . . . Jennifer, it's not really for me to say, but I wondered . . . Jennifer, I know you're fully capable of passing the entrance exam, but . . .'

She couldn't seem to get started on it. She was feeling too angry with the girl's father to be tactful. She decided she'd better leave it for now. They got to the castle gate and she turned to her, and said, 'Here you are then,' but Jennifer looked upset, and said, 'Can't I come to the airfield with you?' and Miss Ellie said, 'Sure. Of course. If you're not expected at home yet. Why not.' And then they did have a talk, but it wasn't about Jennifer's secondary school choices. It was about Piper.

When they got to the bus Piper had got the babies lined up with their backs turned. They each had a long tail made of string, and cardboard ears fixed to their heads with stretchy hairbands. They looked weird. When the minibus came to a halt they all turned round – they had whiskers painted onto their cheeks – and they began to sing.

'run after the farmer's wife . . .'

Shrill little voices. Miss Ellie was still clambering down from the driver's seat – she had a touch of sciatica – when Jazz blurted out, 'My dad says the town can't pay you.'

'. . . *carving knife* . . .'

'He says you've got no sense of civic responsibility. He says you're creepy.'

'. . . *see such a thing in your life* . . .'

Miss Ellie said, 'Hush, Jennifer, we agreed didn't we …' but Jazz, who'd been so grown up and self-possessed in the mini-bus, was sobbing and sobbing and Piper knelt down and held his arms out and she ran and hugged him, and all the little mice came and clung on around her so that it looked as though Piper's head was sticking out of the top of a child-mountain, and he patted Jazz's back, and said, 'That's what your dad, says, is it? And I guess no one put a hand up to contradict?'

He looked very hard at Miss Ellie as he said it and she looked away and began plaiting the woollen strings of her cardigan.

Piper was quiet for a while. Then he pulled his mouth into a blowing shape, as though he was whistling without sound, and he said to the musical mice, 'Come on, kiddywinks, let's see if we can make Jennifer laugh,' and they all began to run around her on all fours, with their bottoms in the air and their string tails switching, and they wrinkled up their noses and showed their little teeth and went squeak squeak squeak until Jazz let go of Piper. Then he said, to her and to Elsa and to all of them, 'I think . . . perhaps . . . in view of what Jennifer's father says . . . in that case . . . after all . . . I will play tomorrow,' and they all shouted out 'Hooray!'

*   *   *

The town's main car park was an amorphous space between the Thoroughfare and the river. There were lines on the tarmac to show you how to park in neat rows, but no one paid attention to them. It was a place of dustbins and abandoned bicycles, and when the wind blew the plastic bottles rolled back and forth, as though searching for an exit. When the bright red double-decker bus trundled in it was as though a light had been switched on on a dreary evening, or as though some enormous gaudy beast had slunk into town.

'I didn't know that thing could still move,' said Elsa's dad, as he dropped her off at her mum's house. Elsa's mum was terribly thin now, with raw red patches on her face and hands, but she still kept saying she could cope. He didn't know how he was ever going to persuade her to let him have the girly more often. She looked vague. She said, 'Piper's a pretty good mechanic. Everyone says.'

They stood together and stared as the bus reversed neatly into a space by the entrance. They both thought about the row they'd had the summer before last when their house and garden were full of ants, and when he thought she was seeing too much of the exterminator. They'd said awful words. And afterwards, although it had been a ridiculous fuss about nothing, they couldn't settle back down together again, not with those words clawing at their minds. Now she knew he'd like to help more, he was a good man, but she couldn't risk letting him see her when she was all undone by pain and terror, not now she couldn't trust his love.

Piper was wearing his funny trousers. They'd become his trademark. He crossed the road and walked into the gardens by the river, with his saxophone slung over his shoulder. His hair was glossy and slicked up in a quiff, and the toes of his pony-hide boots were pointed and long. He didn't stare about at the stripy tents where beaded headbands and dream-catchers were sold, at the food-stalls, or at the crowds of townspeople. He bought a pint and settled down at a little metal table outside the beer tent. When people he knew walked past – and he knew most people – he greeted them by lifting his eyebrows and giving a slight nod. No one sat down beside him, although there was an extra plastic chair.

When the Blondie cover band started playing, all the women crammed into the big tent and put their arms up and rocked from side to side like wobbly-men. There were a lot of children about, and the fathers sat with them on their laps, or bought them hot dogs. The small ones darted in and out of the light like midges, tiny Elsa tagging along. Grandparents brought out their folding chairs and thermoses and sat with their backs to the bands.

Jazz came in with some other big girls, all of them dressed alike in sequined vests and tight white jeans. She was wearing lipstick. She looked at Piper shyly, and walked on by.

Sylvia would have sat with Piper. She'd been wanting to see him, but Billy had a really high temperature. She kept dialling the locum but the woman just said Paracetamol, keep him warm, plenty of fluids, as though Sylvia didn't already know all that. It was insulting. She wasn't going to get any help. All she could do was be with him.

She lay on the big bed – Billy'd begged to sleep with her – and stared at the ceiling listening to the odd inhuman sound of his snoring and smelling the illness on his breath. It wasn't that the music was particularly good, but the sound of a party from which one has been excluded is desolating. Sylvia began to cry quietly, because she was frightened for Billy, and because she thought, That's it. Nothing new is ever going to happen to me again. She went to sleep, and snored too. She missed the whole drama. When she woke the next morning with her clothes still on, she thought – for the first and only time – How lucky I am that my precious baby's deaf.

Afterwards no one could quite remember how it happened that Piper, who wasn't listed on the programme, got to be playing on the main stage. He was just suddenly there, flapping his left hand imperiously at the sound-man. That was Johnny from the garage: when he didn't get enough GCSEs for college, Piper had taught him all about music tech in exchange for a summer's worth of fuel and maintenance. The women tugged their tops down and their trousers up and laughed at each other for no reason but that dancing made them feel like giddy girls again, and when Piper launched into the riff, some of the men came out of the beer tent, and put their bottles down, and paired off and began to jive.

The band whose set had been interrupted looked nonplussed for a bar or two and then the drummer picked up the beat and the lead guitarist began to do the duck-walk. (How many hours, how many hundreds and hundreds of hours, it seemed like, had he spent practising it in front of his mother's floor-length mirror.)

The girl in the song had inordinate appetites and seven-league boots. Her allure was irresistible. She was a juvenile, sweet silly sixteen, but she had the adults gyrating around her like hungry rodents. Everybody had heard about Chuck Berry's transgressions. But everybody, for now at least, was swaying to his fable of the greedy teenaged nymphet.

Piper was rocking forth and back like the figurehead of a ship in a deeply furrowed sea. His hair was a plumed copper helmet. His boot-heels rapped on the flimsy staging. His sax glittered and so did his sharp pale eyes. By the end of 'Maybellene' the beer tent was empty. He swung the sexes in together with a medley of the songs they'd courted to. He'd laid the sax down gently and taken the mike. The singer stripped his vest off, revealing a chest all over mapped in blue, and began to do back-flips.

Big men were finding frail little wives, and tremendously breasted women were laying hands on whippety-thin husbands, and couples who hadn't really given each other a thought in years were mouthing declarations of passion along with Piper's wheedling baritone. They wanted, they crooned, to hold each other's hands. They yearned for each other eight days a week. The women put their forearms on the men's shoulders and let hands coarsened by washing-up and potato-scrubbing dangle while they pressed their soft well-used bellies to their husbands' belt-buckles.

The two young women from Franklin's were up on the stage harmonising with Piper. They both sang in the choir, Sundays, but, Saturday nights, they sang folk-songs a cappella, their high voices uncanny and penetrating.

Down on the trampled turf of the dance-floor the men looked sheepish, and then lascivious, and buried their faces in their women's necks and the women let their eyelids droop, so that they didn't see how the children had come creeping out of shrubberies where bushes formed caves, and from dens behind log-piles and from secret places down by the river where the bank did a jink and left exposed a pebbled beach big enough for two boys to lie smoking or, on this night, slyly, shyly running their fingers through each other's hair because there was something narcotic and bewitching about the way Piper sang.

The children crept together. They didn't approach the stage, where their parents were leaning propped against each other, sustained by sentimentality and lust and a rapturous feeling that this Piper, for all that preposterous demand he'd made, was . . . well, what was he . . . a man who could make a party go, a pretty decent singer when all's said and done, a bit special.

The Polish builders (or were they Romanian? Nobody knew) who lived in the mildewed caravan on the airfield, next to Piper, were up on stage too now, one with a harmonica, the other with a keyboard so tiny he could tuck it under his arm. Black-nails stepped forward to take the mike. Piper let her. He picked up the sax again and made it hum softly as she belted out 'White Rabbit'.

The children formed a phalanx, well back in the gloaming, quite a distance from where their parents smooched and swayed. Black-nails's voice was tremendous. As she let it blare out (Smiler weaving treble harmonies around it) Piper sidled offstage. His saxophone still sang softly, but no one could see where he'd got to. No one was really looking. There was a shuffling and a rustling and a quiet and swift evacuation.

The adult couples let their heads drop back and their eyes close as they chanted at the canvas roof. They were young again and high and totally irresponsible. They'd forgotten that once you're a parent you must never ever forget the fact, not even for a second, not even for the winking of an eye or a shake of a mouse's tail.

The bus went by along the riverside road towards the sea. All its interior lights were on. It was a mirage. It had to be. It wasn't Piper's beat-up old wreck, with all the seats out. It was a proper double-decker bus, with a powerful if air-polluting diesel engine, and a pair of animated children waving from each window – upstairs and down.

Humphrey Leach was standing by the gate into the gardens. He had come looking for Jennifer to remind her that he'd be leaving at 6 a.m. prompt for an executive-level brainstorming away-day and if she really wanted a lift to Ipswich, as she'd said, then she'd be better be home in bed spit-spot. He saw his daughter standing up in the brilliantly illuminated bus next to the copper-haired driver. She wore a gold-braided cap and leather cross-belts, a satchel on one hip, a ticket puncher on the other. She caught his eye and waved as the bus swept by. It never came back.

'People-trafficking,' said someone later that night. But the word didn't quite seem to fit.

Abduction. Kidnapping. Those words weren't right either. They jarred with the picture they all had in their heads, that of the children's faces, lit up with happiness as they waved from the bus.

They'd jumped in their cars and raced after, of course they had. The police had been on to it right away. But the bus seemed to have dematerialised. There was not a trace of it, not a tyre track, not a broken twig. Several of the men went down to the Ness with torches, but the tide was high and there was nothing to be seen but smooth flowing water. 'That bus is like fifteen feet tall,' said Elsa's father. His voice was muffled and cracked. 'You can drown a rat here, but you can't lose a London bus.' They knew he was right, but they stayed with him until dawn. When one or other of them began to sob, awful wracking man-sobs – the others would pass him cigarettes, or sucky sweets. When the sea had drained right out, and the river dwindled back to a liquid snake writhing through its narrow channel, there was nothing to be seen there, not a jelly-shoe or a scrunchie or a flossy-maned pink plastic pony – just the long-legged birds poking around in the weeds and bubbles burping their way to the surface of the smooth grey mud.

Elsa's mother stopped the treatment. She said she didn't see the point of doing herself in for the sake of a few more months of life, not when life was so futile and sad. No one could blame her. Her husband got together with Sylvia after a while, and they took Billy away to a bigger place, where there were other children. He never really played with the others much, though. Eventually his mother gave in and let him have a pet rat. He called it Elsa, and every time he murmured to it his stepfather looked around sharply, and then looked away. They seldom had music in the house.

Humphrey Leach moved on too. He was promoted to senior area manager and had to give up the castle and move into the county town. He and his thin girlfriend lived on the eighth floor of a converted warehouse overlooking the old docks. There was a gym in the basement, and that was a plus, but neither of them slept well there, and neither ever told the other that all night long they heard scuffling and chattering as a hidden horde of creatures went about their business within the cavity wall. Humphrey's career stalled. 'You're a safe pair of hands, Leach,' said the CEO, 'and we all value that, but we're looking for more of a people-person.' It was a woman who got the next promotion. 'She's kind, isn't she?' said one junior executive to another (they weren't called secretaries any more). Humphrey, overhearing, was nonplussed. No one on his business diploma course had ever mentioned kindness as being a useful character trait.

After a few years rumours began to reach the town of a bus that turned up at festivals, or on Cornish beaches. There were a load of young people who lived on it. They dressed up and performed puppet shows and made wood-carvings of small animals. They cooked curries and paellas in enormous tureens and sold them to hungry dancers. Whatever was left over at the end of the night they gave away. They were musicians – folkies mainly, but there was an old jazzer with them. The bus was called Ratty – nobody knew why.

These ancient fables have many variants and ramifications. The summaries that follow include only those parts of them echoed in the stories in this book.

Orpheus

Orpheus was a musician whose singing was so beautiful it could shift rocks and tame wild beasts. His wife Eurydice died and was dragged down into the Underworld. Orpheus followed her there, gaining access to the realm of the dead by the power of his music. He pleaded with Hades, King of the Underworld, and his wife, Persephone. Moved by his singing, they agreed Eurydice could follow Orpheus back to life, but he was warned that he must not look back at her as they travelled towards the light. He turned. He looked. She died a second time, and for ever.

Actaeon

Diana was the virgin goddess of wild animals and of hunting. Out hunting in the woods, the hero Actaeon chanced upon Diana bathing, naked, surrounded by her nymphs. Angered by his intrusion, the goddess transformed him into a stag. In that form, he was torn apart by his own hounds.

Psyche

Psyche, whose name means 'mind', was a mortal woman so lovely and amiable that Venus, the goddess of love, grew envious of her and instructed her son Cupid to humiliate the girl by making her fall in love with a monster. On seeing Psyche, Cupid fell in love with her. Disregarding his mother's orders, he bore Psyche off to an enchanted palace where he visited her each night, in pitch-darkness, telling her that they could be happy together so long as she never insisted on seeing him. One night, as Cupid slept, Psyche lit a lamp. When she saw his wings, and realised he was a god, she was so startled that she let a drop of hot oil fall from the lamp onto his shoulder. He woke and flew away.

Pasiphae

Pasiphae was the wife of Minos, the legendary king of Crete. When a mysterious bull appeared on the beach Pasiphae was seized with desire for it. She confided in Daedalus, the great architect and inventor, and he made a cow-like contraption for her. Climbing inside it, Pasiphae coupled with the bull. The resulting baby, the Minotaur, had the body of a man but the head of a bull. Daedalus constructed the labyrinth – a maze of underground tunnels – as a prison for it.

One of King Minos's sons was killed in Athens: as compensation Minos demanded that twelve young Athenians should be sent to Crete each year and fed to the Minotaur.

For Ariadne, the daughter of Minos and Pasiphae, Daedalus made a dancing floor. For himself he made wings, and flew away to Egypt.

Joseph

Joseph was a native of Bethlehem but worked as a carpenter in Nazareth. When he found that the young woman whom he was to marry, Mary, was already pregnant, he considered rejecting her. She told him she was a virgin, and that her baby had been miraculously conceived by the agency of the Holy Ghost. The marriage went ahead.

About the time the baby was due the authorities decreed that all immigrants should return to their own birthplaces for registration. Joseph took Mary to Bethlehem. They were homeless there. The baby, Jesus, was born in the temporary accommodation of a stable.

Mary Magdalen

One of Jesus's female followers, she has traditionally been identified with another unnamed biblical character – a 'sinful woman', a prostitute.

Once, when he was weary, she came to where Jesus was seated and washed his feet, and wept over them, and rubbed them with an expensive ointment, and dried them with her hair. When someone rebuked her for wasting money on such a luxury Jesus defended her, 'And he said unto her, thy sins are forgiven.'

On the Friday of the crucifixion Mary Magdalen was among the women gathered at the foot of the cross.

Before sunrise on the following Sunday she went to the place where Jesus was laid. Looking into the tomb, she saw that his body was no longer there. Someone approached her.

Initially she thought he was a gardener. Then she recognised him as the risen Christ.

She reached out. He said, 'Noli me tangere' – Touch me not.

John, in his gospel, repeatedly describes himself as 'the disciple whom Jesus loved'.

Tristan

When King Mark of Cornwall was to marry the Irish princess Isolde he sent his nephew, Tristan, to escort her over the sea to his home. In the course of the journey Isolde's attendant, Brangwyn, gave her a love-potion. Isolde shared it with Tristan and the two fell deeply, ecstatically, helplessly in love. Isolde married Mark, but she and Tristan were driven to seek each other out.

In some tellings of the story King Mark surprises them embracing, and he, or one of his knights, kills Tristan with a poisoned weapon. Isolde dies with him, of a broken heart, or more poison. In other versions Tristan wanders off, joins King Arthur's court, and falls in love with another lady, Isolde of the White Hands.

Piper

When the Saxon town of Hamelin was infested with rats a stranger in particoloured clothing appeared and offered, for a fee, to rid the town of the creatures. The price was shockingly high but the mayor agreed. The stranger brought out a pipe and began to play. The rats, fascinated by the music, followed him out of town. He led them to a river, where they all drowned. The piper returned to Hamelin for his payment. The mayor began to quibble, offering a much smaller sum. The piper left in a rage.

One Sunday, when the adults of the town were all in church, the piper returned and began to play his pipe again. All the children of the town followed him, as the rats had done. He led them away, perhaps to drown in the river, perhaps to disappear into a cave in the side of a mountain. Only one boy, who was too lame to follow the others, or too deaf to hear the bewitching music, was left behind in Hamelin.

ABOUT THE AUTHOR

LUCY HUGHES-HALLETT IS the author of a novel, *Peculiar Ground*, and *The Pike: Gabriele D'Annunzio, Poet, Seducer and Preacher of War*, which won the Samuel Johnson Prize, the Duff Cooper Prize, the Political Book Awards Political Biography of the Year, and the Costa Biography Award. Before that she wrote *Cleopatra: Histories, Dreams and Distortions* and *Heroes: Saviours, Traitors and Supermen*, both of which were published to wide acclaim. *Cleopatra* won the Fawcett Prize and the Emily Toth Award. Lucy lives in London.